athy: I luz
a Merr
and   ᵔᵕᵔy
                ♡

MW01611052

In From the Cold

By

Carole T. Beers

W & B Publishers
USA

W & B Publishers

For information:
W & B Publishers
9001 Ridge Hill Street
Kernersville, NC 27284

www.a-argusbooks.com

ISBN: 9781635541960

Book Cover designed by Cheryl Taylor
Book Cover photo by LouJean Bailey
Printed in the United States of America

0THER BOOKS BY THIS AUTHOR

"Ghost Ranch"

"Night Rides"

"Over The Edge"

"Saddle Tramps"

"Shadow on the River"

Acknowledgments

This heartwarming tale was inspired by a real-life story told me by late author and writing-group mentor, Tim Wohlforth. Knowing of my passion for horses and good yarns, Tim kept insisting I go meet an old horse that a friend of his rescued after spotting it on a drive past a snowy mountainside. It now lived at Equamor, a horse-rescue facility in Ashland, Ore.

When I met the grizzled equine and its rescuer, and toured the enchanting ranch, I fell in love. I immediately had a run at a fictional story keyed by the horse. Then I added a more characters and parallel plot lines. The novella lay in a drawer for five years.

When readers suggested I write a holiday novella, I remembered I had one almost ready to go. Also, a delightful photo by reader Donamae Klausen that would make a perfect cover. It took more time and work than expected (what else is new?) to pull it together. But the book is out, and advocating for all who give and deserve the healing power of mercy.

P.S. "Survivor" died of old age ago at Equamor. But I like to think he died happy with friends all around. Part proceeds from this book's go to Equamor and other animal-rescue programs.

Dedication:

For Mark, Melissa and Dolly. Those who are loved are never lost.

Second chances enrich those who offer them as much—or more—as those who receive them.

Jack

1.

Jack Pennington fought to stay awake and keep his F-350 on the snow-packed road that early December morning. Squeezing the steering wheel rhythmically for something to do, he glanced in the rearview mirror. Staring back at him were baggy, Robert Redford-blue eyes topped by frosty eyebrows under a worn gray Stetson.

Not getting any younger, he thought. *The trip's not getting any shorter, either.*

Pines jutted from both sides of a half-pipe of snow blanketing the highway and shoulders. The trees were only slightly darker than the sky. The asphalt itself was an iced-over washboard where a speed of forty MPH was pushing it.

Jack gave a low "hmmn, hmmn" chuckle. He believed that even in his sleep he could drive this twisty Greensprings Highway from the Rogue Valley to Klamath Basin. No sweat. Hell, he might be asleep right now.

He was getting too old for this. As his wife, Ellen, often reminded him, thirty-five years with Southern Oregon Ag Supply in Ashland was plenty. Especially when you had to drive this old gnarly highway a dozen times a year in all weather, and then drive more when you got to K-Falls. Only to come sideways, once you arrived, with some beet-faced bozo about a botched order of fencing, pipe or feeders.

Klamath Falls had fine ag supply outfits of its own. But there were always the yahoos, all hat and not many cattle, who thought SOAS carried a newer, fancier product. For them it was all about the image, all about the brand. But even longtime ranchers gave him grief.

Whatever, as some of Jack's former foster kids used to say. And still said, far as he knew. At least Carly said it. That sweet kid was the last youngster he and Ellen had taken in—and then bid farewell to when she got herself pregnant and took off with a fat, moody lad who drank, roughed her up once, and couldn't even hold down a job at Taco Temple.

What had Carly seen in him? How had Jack and Ellen failed? And now the young woman was on her own, with a toddler to care for. A troubled boy, at that. With her too proud to ask for help. And stubborn. A little like Jack, come to think of it. At least that's what Ellen claimed.

Jack took a gander at his sleeping passenger, a smelly red-heeler named Green. In a fit of contrariness he'd named the dog for red's opposite color. Mainly since the mutt was the opposite of what a heeler *should* be: Rather than herding livestock, Green let livestock herd him.

"So, Green," Jack ventured, done ruminating on the letter he'd received saying he'd be laid off because the ag outfit was downsizing. Which he took as corporate-speak for his having turned 65. "Whatcha think, boy, about my putting on slippers every day instead of boots, and trading the ol' truck for a rocking chair?"

The dog flicked an ear but continued snoring like a chainsaw.

Jack turned his attention back to the road. He cranked open the window, letting in a whoosh of winter wind. Maybe the roar and biting air would keep him awake.

A long bare section of pavement came into view fifty feet ahead.

He stepped on the gas, held tight to the wheel and manhandled the truck over the chunked ice toward the ice-free stretch. The engine backfired, and then settled into a satisfying roar. The chained-up tires found purchase. He'd make up time and be only minutes late for the sales call.

But you never knew. One minute you were sailing along, your eyes on the road but your mind wondering if the old nag you'd seen in the meadow on other trips this year was still there.

The next minute your tires caught ice and you got pitched headfirst into a snowbank or, in open spots like this where you accelerated, were flung halfway down a mountain.

Jack recalled how two years ago he'd rescued a wiry old hunter in a veteran's cap who took a turn too fast and launched his Jeep into trees below. The guy seemed disoriented, as if he'd suffered a concussion but refused to let Jack take him to a hospital. He just wanted to go home. Which is where Jack took him—subsequently kicking himself for not having the man checked out. The next week The Ashland Tidings carried a death notice for an old Navy man who died of injuries suffered days earlier in a crash off this vey road.

Now, whenever Jack saw an aged veteran on the street or at the grocery, he thought of this. He hadn't served in the military, rejected for having flat feet. But he never saw what that had to do with his ability to fight, or serve his country a different way.

Rounding a turn onto another straightaway, Jack relaxed his grip on the wheel. He eased his foot off the gas. His gaze swept the white and gray landscape to his right where a sparsely treed slope flattened into a trackless meadow framed by far timber.

He tried to focus on his driving. But that became harder when anxiety squeezed his chest.

Would he see that old brown bronc again? As he had one pewter day the previous December, and on other runs he'd made that spring, summer and fall? It had become an anticipated landmark. But it was also much more. The horse was a beacon of hope.

2.

Jack recalled when he'd first spotted the animal. It was shortly after last winter's record blizzard. As he entered this same stretch of road, his gaze had slid down to the right where a blocky shape stood out in the snowscape. A weak sun trying to penetrate thick clouds cast an eerie spotlight there.

In pooled light stood a dark horse, sway backed, woolly as a mammoth. It stood with its head bowed and tail to the wind near a mound of brambles a hundred yards off the highway. A dusting of snow defined its sunken top line. Wind ruffled its mane.

It could have been a statue. From up here it had looked like a toy—a rusted trotting horse like one his wife had set near a wagon wheel by their front porch. In snow reaching its knees and hocks, with more flakes blowing sideways, this real horse stood motionless. Only silvered puffs rhythmically spouting from its nose showed it was alive.

Jack had felt a stab of pity. The horse was aged. Its shape and posture were proof of that. Jack wondered if it suffered from dementia, injury or illness, and had wandered up here from a ranch in the valley to die alone. Some livestock did that.

Or had it been driven off by its herd mates? It could not be a wild or feral equine. There were no true wild horses in these parts. There never really had been—at least in modern times. Too high, too little forage, too many cougar and coyote. Not to mention trigger-happy hunters.

Jack had not slowed or stopped on that drive last winter. He figured the horse was none of his business. It probably had been there awhile and could take care of itself in snowy weather. It could browse on brambles as did deer, and paw through snow to eat winter-cured grass and lick that same snow for water. The horse had the bramble for cover, and, worst case, distant trees.

He hadn't slowed then. But on subsequent journeys Jack took to looking for the old horse in the meadow. To his relief it was always there. Sometimes near the tree line, other times out in the open, occasionally half-hidden by the long blackberry thicket.

The animal became a beacon. It broke up what, for Jack, had become a predictably dull and unsatisfying grind of work, chores and a stalled marriage. If the horse were still there and alive, all was right with the world. It meant it had survived the odds and was still in its place, surviving by the grace of what? A higher power? Nature at least. Jack took it to mean that he, saddled with relatively puny troubles and complaints, could survive, too.

On a trip earlier this Spring, when he spotted the horse pawing at tufts that poked through snow a hundred feet from the road, Jack did slow the truck. He pulled into a wide space along the road and let the engine idle so he could really study the animal.

That's when he saw it was a gelding. Probably a former ranch gelding, a reliable mount that had trailed, herded and separated cattle, maybe dragged calves to the fire for doctoring and branding. The horse itself might in fact wear a brand.

Jack wriggled sideways in his seat, rolling down the window for a better look. His left elbow hit the steering wheel center pad. The truck horn blared rudely in the pristine stillness.

The horse jerked up his head. Then he jumped sideways, neck like a periscope, and turned to face the truck, with breaths like smoke signals billowing up from his nostrils.

His eyes looked directly into Jack's. The dark brown orbs, rimmed with white, questioned and challenged. They showed intelligence. That chestnut face itself, marked by a large star and snip, was extravagantly grizzled. The head was long with strong jowls and a Roman nose.

He's more proud than pretty.

The stout legs were feathered with thick winter guard-hairs, like those of a draft horse. Yet this horse had a certain lightness and dignity about him. Jack decided he'd once been passably handsome, secure in his looks and purpose.

Horse and man stayed that way a long moment, taking each other's measure. Then the horse spun, bucked like a colt and bolted for the timber.

This particular snowbound morning, two months since he'd last seen the horse and eight months after that mutually aware encounter, Jack again swung the truck through packed, red-gravel-pocked snow onto the shoulder. He aimed for the wide spot where he could pull over. Tapping the brake, he halted the truck.

When he looked out over the meadow again, cold fear gripped his heart. The horse was not there. He looked again. The horse was gone. No sign of him.

"Old boy's not here, Green."

The dog opened one eye and then closed it again.

Jack slumped in his seat. What had happened? Did the animal find his way back home, or had he been brought back to the ranch by his owner? Or had a predator or some juked-up, trigger-happy hunter picked the gelding off?

Maybe, challenged by increasing age and exposure, the old geezer had just cantered off to that great grassy meadow in the sky to join with lost herd mates.

Yeah, right. And I'm the king of Romania.

Jack opened the door. Holding onto the cab frame, he climbed out to stand on the truck's running board for a better look. He might even step down and go around the truck. He had to relieve himself, anyway.

When one of his feet hit the ground, a tractor-trailer going full bore roared by, gears grinding, chains clanking on packed snow and bare pavement. Dirty slush and ice slammed Jack's cheek and torso. Ice stung his neck and melted under his collar.

Half-blinded, he shook his head and spat out curses that would make his even his world-wise wife blush. Then he brushed himself off, re-set his Stetson and got down off the running board. He also let out Green, who immediately raised a leg against a tire.

Jack stumbled through hard snow to a white-mantled thicket. Stopping there to let Nature take its course, Jack occupied his mind with hopes the geezer horse had indeed found its way home to some ranch in the valley.

That's what he wanted to believe. But Jack also began to think that if he did see the horse again, if it were still here, he would need to do something. No, he would *have* to do something. The animal would be even more challenged this year. This first blizzard was harsh enough. But even more severe storms were fore-cast.

Climate change not only is real, he thought for the umpteenth time. It's breaking down our door. How would that old horse make it through another year? If predators, old age, Arctic winds and exposure didn't kill him, thirst and starvation surely would.

Finishing his business, Jack whistled the dog back and they picked their way through red-gravel flecked snow to the truck. He scanned the meadow from this different viewpoint. His gaze came to rest on the bramble pile. It looked bigger. His pulse skipped.

There was the horse.

Calm settled over Jack. He relaxed his shoulders and listened to the wind. It blew without ceasing, now harder, now lighter. But it was always there, biting, enervating. He shrugged deeper into his lumberjack coat, and patted the dog.

"He's still here, Green," Jack said. "Damn! He's a tough one."

The dog looked up and cocked his head. Then he whined and gave his tail a weak wag.

"I know, boy. It's cold. Get in the truck." He opened the door and the dog sprang in.

Jack lingered a moment longer. He could make out only two dark ears and a ruffled mane through gaps in the brambles. But the horse was out there. That was the main thing. Regular streams of expelled air rose from the gelding's head.

Joy surged through Jack. He stood holding his own breath, craving an even sharper view. But it was too cold to stay in that place very long. He knocked the snow off his boots and climbed into the 350.

Back in the cab smelling of oily rags and old dog, he unscrewed the top of his dented steel thermos and sipped the bitter but still-warm coffee. His toes felt so cold that even his tattered, flannel-lined slippers at home wouldn't have warmed them.

Jack vowed that as soon as he got back from this trip, tomorrow or the day after, he would try to locate the horse's owner.

He just had to find some way to help that old bronc. That's what you did for one in need, whether a person or an animal. That's what he and Ellen had done for years for a handful of hollow-eyed kids they'd rescued from hopeless homes. Or rather, *lack* of homes.

That's what Jack hoped, when the time came, someone would do for him.

Carly

3.

What was that noise?

Bam, bam, bam!

Still half-lost in her studies, Carly Brown glanced up from her textbook on the dining table. She stared at the cuckoo clock, a gift from her former foster parents, Daddy Jack and Mama Ellen. It bonged and cuckooed eight times.

The hammering continued, and the *zoftig* twenty-year-old with pink-streaked hair looked around her studio apartment, pleased with her attempts to brighten it up for the holidays. Her gaze jumped to her three-year-old pounding a cell phone on the floor by the Christmas tree.

"Mikey! Stop!" Carly smacked her hand on the table and prepared to haul her hundred-sixty pounds to her feet.

The boy didn't stop. He didn't even appear to have heard.

Carly swiped her hair out of her lined eyes and slammed down her other hand, upending her takeout-coffee mug. She watched as a milky brown pool spread to the edge of her book and trickled toward her purple sweats.

"What the...eff." She caught herself in time; the boy didn't need to hear such words. She whipped the book from further harm, leaned over and shook her head while madly mopping the table with her sweat-shirt sleeves.

It's a good thing my laptop was across the table, or I'd probably ruin that, too.

The mopping sent her last good Sharpie flying toward the tree—a pre-lit job she'd scored for five bucks at Past Perfect thrift store near the Ashland suburb of Talent, now her home.

Her cheeks flamed. She struggled to raise herself off her creaky chair. But the chair had other ideas, tipping precariously and then bouncing back. Its knife-edge rungs stung her calves.

"Damn!" She rubbed the back of her legs. "Now look what you made Mommy do." Hearing herself as if from afar, hating her overreaction, she forced her voice into a calmer mode. "Put down the phone, baby. Come on. Do it now."

"No good," said Mike. He was a tiny untattoed version his darkly handsome father, currently MIA. "Get new, get new one." He rocked back and forth on his knees.

Surprise flooded Carly. An unexpected rush of happiness. And boy, could she use some of that now. Troubled though Mikey was, agitated and wild, or dull and stony, the boy was also making sense tonight. Trying to communicate. Were his meds finally working?

She allowed a pinspot of hope to glow in her mind. This might be the start of a more promising year for her son. For her, as well.

"Mommy can't afford a new phone, Mikey. We have to be nice to that one." She lowered her shoulders and wondered if these words made any sense to him.

The boy looked down and stroked the phone.

Miracle of Miracles. Have I gotten through?
"I'll get you a cookie, Mister Mike. Your favorite. Chocolate-chip oatmeal. Look at your animal picture-book, if you need something to do. There's a good boy." She limped to the sofa bed, picked up "Our Animal Friends," and handed it to him with one hand while smoothing his ruffled hair with the other.

The boy looked at her flatly. His black eyebrows disappeared under long bangs. He either had not heard, or had not understood what she'd just said.

Which was it? Carly never knew. But she had learned to accept that, and to try another approach. That's what the therapist said to do.

Without warning Mikey threw the phone into the tree.

Ka-thunk!

The dubious evergreen wobbled on its base, lights winking, colorful ornaments clicking.

Carly's pinspot of hope dimmed. Darkness dropped over her like a shroud.

"Mike! You're driving me crazy." Heart hammering, she steadied herself with one hand on arm of the the sofa bed.

The boy sat up abruptly. He stared at the still-quivering tree.

Ashamed of her outburst, Carly got control her shaking body and again softened her tone. "If you don't behave, I'm gonna tell Gampy Jack. Santa, too. You don't want me to do that, do you? They might not bring presents."

Mikey's lower lip trembled. He fixated on the wall. Fear drifted over his face like clouds over the moon.

Even that was too harsh. But I am near the end of my rope.

Trying to think how to make the best of things, Carly busied herself picking strands of hair free from where they'd caught in her finger rings. Then she reached toward her son.

Mikey dropped onto all fours and skittered around the tree. His movements sent a green-glass ball crashing to the floor. While shiny splinters fanned out from impact, he scrambled out from under a quivering branch and launched himself, back first, onto the sofa bed. Thumb in mouth, he folded into a fetal position.

Carly watched him with tenderness and uncertainty. This was getting to be more than she could handle. What made her think that she—a virtually friendless average girl from troubled circumstances—could study hard, get Certified Nursing Assistant jobs, and improve her life while being a good mom to a special-needs child?

She walked over and touched Mikey's back. When he didn't pull away, she stroked it, and then gave him a short, light hug.

He felt stiff and hot. But he grunted softly.

Acceptance.

Carly went to the kitchenette on the other side of the table. Drawing two cookies from a jar, she returned and offered one to the boy. He looked at it. She let herself believe he registered her offering at some level, maybe even saw it as a peace offering.

But that was just a guess. There was no way to know how he processed things.

She adjusted the boy's position so he lay on his back. She pulled a knitted throw over him and tucked a cookie in one of his hands. When he pushed it into his mouth, chewed, and swallowed, Carly felt her blood pressure drop. She retrieved her Sharpie and returned to her book.

The chair's legs screeched as she pulled it farther out from the table. Still sore from its earlier attack, she eyed it suspiciously. Then, with a weak grin, she sat down.

If things were ever going to improve for her and Mikey, she absolutely had to concentrate on her studies. Doing well, passing the exam to be a level-one nursing assistant, was her way out. Thank goodness Daddy Jack had advanced her money for classes and books.

She knew she shouldn't get so angry, yell at her kid that way. He was different. But he had to learn to listen. What if he were in danger, like when a dog threatened him or a car was coming? What if Mike needed to pay attention, like, right now?

Carly also needed for Mikey to be quiet and not act out when she was studying. The CNA exam was coming up within days. The one she'd had to leave early last summer when a babysitter called in a panic to say Mikey had pulled a chest of drawers onto himself.

Luckily, his injuries were minor.

Carly just had to pass the test this time. Doing so would help her get good-paying jobs. In fact she already tentatively had a job lined up with a lady with cerebral palsy, in Ashland. Solid work, and not at places like Taco Temple, would rescue her and Mikey from their whirlpool of need and dependence. Not to mention, shame.

Carly could get off welfare. Buy her own groceries with real money, not food stamps, and leave the food banks for people worse off than she. Could be her own woman. Independent. No longer a drag on society, but a credit to it. Mikey would grow up in a productive, positive home.

I can be a helper rather than a helpee. Is there even such a word as helpee?

A smirk quirked her lips.

At least I've still got my sense of humor.

Just as important, earning her own money would enable Carly to move beyond verbally thanking Daddy Jack, her ex-foster father. He'd helped her as a teen when her parents got sick with drugs. Working with a service agency he'd helped her when they were on the street, her parents stealing from strangers—as well as friends and family—to support their habits.

Jack had talked his wife into taking Carly as a foster child, when two others already lived with them. He'd seen something special in her: a spirit for helping others that mirrored his own.

"I don't see what's the big deal about giving a street kid half my candy bar," she'd said. "Or socks I found in the dumpster, and washed."

But he had also recognized her spirit for what it was. "People give for many reasons," he told her. "To obey a religious edict, to impress others. Not everyone has real heartfelt empathy for other beings"—words that made her glow inside.

Daddy Jack extended his hand occasionally even now, though Carly tried not to become too dependent. So her having money would let her pay him back for the courses but also let her show him her gratitude with, say, a fine Christmas gift. Something extra special. Something he would not buy for himself.

Like those hundred-dollar Pendleton sheepskin slippers he'd asked his wife and his adult biological kids for the past few years, but hadn't yet received. Those warm, cushy slippers with rubber soles that could laugh at snow when he wore them on the porch to fetch firewood he'd chopped for the woodstove. Handsome slippers, to keep his ten tender toes toasty.

"Toasty toes," Carly would call him. And he would laugh. Like her, Daddy Jack did enjoy a play on words.

Daddy Jack would never buy such luxury items for himself. Not that he couldn't afford them. He had a job, a house and truck. But he was way too thrifty. He was so tight with money that he still had unworn, gifted Pendleton flannel shirts folded with pins and cardboard in his dresser drawer. He preferred to wear out his older shirts first.

Carly knew this because she sometimes did housework and cooking for him and Mama Ellen when the latter's arthritis kicked up. Which it did a lot these days, and which had forced the kind older woman to rely on others to take her to church and appointments when Jack was away on his business trips to Klamath Basin to sell and deliver farm equipment.

Putting away dishes and doing laundry in the Pennington home, modest though it was compared to fancier homes and condos springing up around Ashland, afforded Carly glimpses into a life she one day hoped to live. No, *planned* on living, with her boy. And hopefully with a second child, should a proper, stay-the-course father materialize.

But foremost on her wish list this holiday, after getting her caregiver's license, was finding some serious help for Mikey.

4.

Her clock bonged twelve. Carly looked up from her textbook to see the cuckoo clock's door pop open and the bird itself jump out and call the midnight hour before snapping back inside his hideaway.

What kind of crazy bird would live in a tiny wooden house with a snapping door?

One who's cuckoo. Ha ha, whatever. To each to his own.

Holding out her long purple nails, and careful not to stab herself or smear her eyeliner, Carly rubbed her burning eyelids.

No one else might see Carly's made-up eyes and nails, or other attempts at looking pretty. But she had to try. Even if you *were* too pear-shaped, pasty-faced and frumpy to fit in with the going-places crowd, you had to try. You had to look like you took yourself seriously so other people would. So you would, too, if you caught your reflection in a mirror or window.

Nate had liked it. In fact he'd sometimes remarked on it, telling her she looked just like a movie star, and treating her to a coffee and deli sandwich after he'd shoveled snow for someone or had a good day panhandling.

What was that loser up to now, this first week after Thanksgiving? Had the dude sobered up, maybe spent turkey-day with his family in Klamath? Or did he still scrabble for odd jobs and handouts on city streets, and camp on the Greenway between Medford and Ashland?

Carly told herself she didn't care one way or the other. It was his life, after all. She had her own life now. And Mikey.

The boy was still napping on the sofa bed, thank God. Face up, an arm thrown across his torso, cookie crumbs dotting his lips. She wanted to sweep him into her arms and kiss the heck out of him. Formally put him to bed. But she needed him quiet for at least another hour, and feared setting him off.

She blinked. The burn in her eyes from all this reading wasn't going away. Her butt ached in the hard oak chair. Her brain cried for a break, as well. Carrying the half-full container of pumpkin spice coffee to the microwave, she nuked it and then brought it back to the table.

It wouldn't hurt to rest a few moments. But only a few. The test was two days away; she had to study like an Einstein on speed. Carly raised the cup for a long swallow. The coffee was too hot, but tasted heavenly, warming her all the way down.

Becoming aware of a classic country tune playing faintly beyond the walls, probably over a car radio or in the next-door apartment—was it George Strait, Daddy Jack's favorite?— she let her gaze wander among pictures of country scenes and animals on the wall. The one of a black stallion prancing in a meadow made her heart race. She loved the idea of horses. They were so strong, pretty and free. But she was scared of them in real life. They were just so huge and unpredictable.

She wished their home was always this peaceful for her and Mkey. Napping, the boy looked normal.

She closed her own eyes, prayed it were so, and re-membered.

Carly had not noticed her son's autism right away. The first years of his life were like those of any other child she knew about. He was just a soft, squishy baby, and now a toddler, with the usual needs, quirky moves and adorable, staring blue eyes.

Why did children's eyes seem so much bigger than adult eyes?

She'd heard somewhere, maybe from Mama Ellen, that it's because children's eyes are adult size at birth, and the body grows up and into them.

Mikey had been a calm infant, even from birth. But he rarely locked eyes with her. When he did, he showed no emotion. He also fussed when held, except when nursing. She worried she was doing something wrong, and cried herself to sleep many a night. When she told people she might be a horrible mom, they said Mikey had a bug, or gas, or was going through a phase.

Carly opened her eyes. She sat by Mike on the so-fa and brushed cookie crumbs off his lips. Her gaze fell on a photo on the side table. It was shot at a park last summer by a stranger using her friend Sukaya's phone. It showed Carly, Mike, and Sukaya and her children near a jungle gym. Green lawns and leafed-out trees filled in the background.

The photo made Carly think of the Sukaya's life-changing words months before.

Words that had to do with how Carly could help Mikey.

A mother of three, Sukaya Jackson lived four apartments over with her aged parents. She said the words one morning when the two of them sat on Car-ly's front steps, and watched their kids play in a pallid spring sun. It was a rare day Sukaya was not caring for other youngsters in her home, delivering papers, or running errands for others. She was a go-getter, that girl. She never suffered from the low self-esteem that sometimes plagued Carly.

Carly had brought coffee and Oreos for them all to snack on. Suky's kids yelled, laughed, and dug like dogs with toy shovels in the front yard. Mikey squatted to one side, staring at a tree root exposed by a crack in the sidewalk by the busy road.

"I still can't get him to play like other kids, though God knows I've tried," Carly said, setting her mug on the porch and wrapping her arms around her knees. "And he still doesn't speak sentences though he knows some words. Hates being held. I feel like such a failure."

Sukaya nodded, her beaded dreadlocks bobbing about her round face. She drank some coffee and then set down her cup. "What does your doctor say?"

"We haven't been to a doctor," said Carly, looking away. "You know, time, money…mainly money. Mikey's been so healthy…"

"I can take you. You know me. Chauffeur to the world." Sukaya smiled at her joke.

"Nice of you to offer. I'll think about it."

Sukaya picked up an Oreo and studied it, her forehead wrinkling. She pulled it apart and licked the filling off one half. "It's gotta be autism. I saw on Oprah it's on the rise. Or autism spectrum." She popped both cookie halves in her mouth.

Carly set her hands on the porch, leaned back and waited for a car with a missing or cracked muffler pass on the street before she spoke.

"I've heard of that but never really knew what it was. So many kids seem to have it these days. Isn't it like an allergy, caused by vaccines?"

Sukaya waved a hand. "Naw. That's old school, girl. Not true. It's more about messed up genes. Nobody's fault. It just happens."

Carly thought about this. "Is that so?"

"Mikey fits the description. You should take him to the public health clinic. Wouldn't cost you anything."

A few days later Carly had done just that.

She remembered the clinic as cold and a little intimidating. But the medical assistant, and then a doctor, had confirmed Suky's guess of Little Mike's condition, and sent him and Carly home with a brochure and referral. Reading this brochure, and other information online, only deepened Carly's depression.

Some advice said to get a puppy or a kitten, to help an autistic child learn empathy, communication and responsibility. Stuctured animal-therapy was thought to be effective.

But Carly couldn't afford a pet then or now, even one from the Animal Control shelter, which had a high adoption fee. However she learned that Southern Oregon Humane Society, supported by donations, was supposed to help with special-needs adopters.

She hadn't gotten around to that, either. She had never been around animals much, except when living with the Penningtons, whose weiner dog always growled at her. Besides. Her apartment complex probably didn't allow them.

At least the referral to a neurologist had resulted in Mikey's being tested and put on meds to level out his moods. The pills had, for a time, seemed to work. In recent weeks he'd shown improvement. He vocalized more. Behaved a little more. Even accepted hugs. She'd allowed herself to think the pills—and her educated parenting—were helping.

But then tonight he had shown, with the cell phone and the tree and his response to her in those panicky moments, that Mikey was, if anything, reverting. Maybe even getting worse.

Had Carly's preoccupation with her studying set him back? She was only trying to do the best for both of them. It wouldn't be for that long. Nobody could blame her for trying to stay healthy, prepare for her test, and give Mike and herself some kind of Christmas.

Christmas. Always a big holiday for her as well as for the Penningtons and their kids, foster and biological. Carols, treats, gatherings by Daddy Jack and Mama Ellen's fire, even church visits to see candles lit and hear inspiring words.

And presents. Always heartwarming, validating presents.

She and Mikey needed presents. Real gifts. Or at least, Mikey did. She could do with whatever came her way. Passing the test would be present enough Carly.

She would try to get a lift, and hit the U.S. Marines' Toys for Tots giveaway the next weekend. Sukaya said they had excellent toys and clothing, all new—unlike at those at thrift stores where, though the items were clean, they sometimes smelled of smoke and mold.

Or the scent of someone else.

Jack

5.

In a farm-store parking lot not far from town, Jack fidgeted in the truck seat. He shut off his cell phone and stashed it in a jacket pocket. No luck this time either, but he had to check anyway. You never knew.

He'd called the sheriff three days ago to report the stranded horse on the pass. They were very nice. They took the information he gave. But they had no reports of a missing horse in that area, or even of one lost farther down the mountain.

Jack sighed, and climbed down from the truck. He looked at the long, low steel building fronted by the Farm Co-op sign. Feeling the chill in his joints, he ambled stiffly over the asphalt to the sliding-glass doors. He paused in the entrance when, on the wall of the exit passage to his left, he saw the bulletin board bristling with flyers.

He squinted across, trying to read the hand-lettered and computer-printout ads, notes and photos. There were lots of puppy and kitten ads, but only one horse ad. It showed a thin, spotted red horse tacked up with a western saddle.

"For Sale," read the flyer. "Price reduced for quick sale. $500 O.B.O."

Yeah, Jack thought, I'll bet. Not many folks like to feed a horse through winter, in these parts and in these tough times. Maybe that's what happened to that old pony on the mountain. Turned out to fend for himself since his owner couldn't afford his keep.

Inside the store, lit with rows of ceiling fluorescents and smelling of leather, chickens and concrete, Jack circled. He picked up Ice-Melt and WD-40, and approached the first sales counter. He leaned his elbows on a snack rack, grabbed a bag of mixed nuts, and then waited for the female customer in front to complete her transaction.

The cashier was a reedy lad with black discs in his earlobes and tattoos snaking out below his tee-shirt arms. He reminded Jack of, who was it, Nate? Carly's former boyfriend? But this guy had way less meat on him. And seemed more "with it." Had a silver cross hanging from a cord around his neck. Nate had worn a silver skull on a chain.

Jack wasn't sure it was Nate, so he chose to say nothing. There still might be bad feelings there. Besides, Jack had other business.

While waiting, he watched the cashier scan a half-dozen red salt blocks and multiple sacks of feed supplements for the tall, athletic-looking woman ahead of him in line. She was pretty in an outdoorsy way. A freckly middle-aged sort of gal in slim jeans, fleece-lined jeans jacket and cowgirl hat. Short, silver brown hair curled out from under the hat.

The woman looked over at Jack. She flashed him a green-eyed grin. He felt a smile and a spoken "Ma'am," welling up in him. But, not wanting conversation, he held his response to a neighborly smile. He nodded, and touched the brim of his cap with one finger.

The woman's acknowledgment gave him a ripple of delight. Didn't get that feeling much anymore. From a stranger, that is. Sometimes he got that sweet, dimpled smile from Ellen, if her arthritis pain wasn't kicking up. But her smile, and the other feelings and touches he'd loved, came less often in recent months. In fact, recent years.

He kept telling Ellen to find some physical activity, preferably outdoors, to help melt off some weight, keep the joints flexible, ease the pain. Just like Ellen kept telling him to go to church. Each of their suggestions went equally ignored.

Ellen used to garden, walk her dogs and occasionally ride a neighbor's horse up in the hills around town. Those activities had kept her younger looking than her actual sixties. They'd kept her able to fit into slim jeans, too.

But the past year or so she had taken to drinking more sodas, eating cookies as if they were going out of style, and wearing voluminous jogging suits—faded blue velour and such.

What had happened? And why?

She claimed not to have the time or inclination for active diversions. She had her church work to do, Meals-on-Wheels deliveries, filling in at the food bank.

Besides, it hurt to exercise, she said. Fibromyalgia accompanied her arthritis. Her CBD oil and mainstream meds kept the pain in check, but just barely.

Jack knew otherwise. Pain, schmain. A light had gone out in her. And so, in him. He didn't know if it were her fault, or even worse, his. So he kept mum.

Now he became aware that the woman in front of him at the farm store had left. In her wake hung a slight horsy scent.

"Sir," said the cashier, "I can help you now, if you're ready."

Jack looked up. The dark young man seemed bright-eyed and cheerful. Probably not a care in the world. At least, comparatively speaking. Jack had felt that way, once.

"Oh, yes, thank you," Jack said, brushing a scrap of paper off the counter. He glanced around. He was the only one in line now. "I'm just buying a few things." He put them down. "What I really need is information."

"I can try to help."

Jack studied the man. So familiar looking, yet not.

"Do you know how I would go about locating the owner of a stray horse?"

"I guess you've called the sheriff," said the man, looking earnest. He leaned on his inked fists, knuckles facing front, on the counter. His eyes were the color of oak leaves in winter.

"Yes," Jack said. "The sheriff has nothing, no leads. Not inclined to help unless there's a clear nuisance, or a danger to others."

"Budget cuts, probably. At least that's what I hear."

"Exactly. But here's the deal. There's a real bad storm forecast, gonna dump way more snow and ice at the higher elevations, and this old horse is stuck by himself up on the pass. I drive by couple times a winter. He's aged a lot. This winter may be his last."

The young man rubbed his jaw. Then he picked up a pen and tapped it on the counter. Like a drummer's stick. Rat-a-tat-tat, rat-a-tat-tat-tat.

Doesn't he know how annoying that is?

"I s'ppose if it really bothers you," the man finally said. "you could take him hay or grain or something. That way you'd know the horse has a good meal at least once in a while."

Jack exhaled, and shook his head. Then he paused. Actually, that wasn't such a bad idea.

"I might just do that," he said. "But I sure would like to find out who owns him and try to return the old guy. Maybe if they can't feed him, they could get a few dollars for him, and let him go to a good home."

The cashier folded his arms. A deep line appeared between his brows.

Jack noticed the young man had, in fact, many wrinkles on his face and neck. As if he were fat and then lost a lot of weight in a hurry. The skin hadn't quite caught up.

"You know he'd be sold to the killers," said the young man. "Hauled to Canada or Mexico? Since there's no more slaughterhouses in the U.S.? If he's as old as you think, no one'd buy him as a riding or work horse."

"You sound like you know the livestock business."

"My uncle runs a cow-calf operation in Klamath."

"Maybe you could call him, then, and see if he knows of anyone missing a ranch horse?"

The cashier nodded.

Jack heard a shopping cart roll up behind him. A cart with a squealing wheel. He saw the cashier glance that way, and then look back at him.

"Well, thanks, anyway," Jack said. "I'd sure appreciate if you would ask around."

"Why don't you put a note on the bulletin board, with your phone number? That way if I or anyone else hears anything, we can let you know."

"Say, I think I'll do just that," Jack said. "Good idea. And Merry Christmas."

"Same to you."

Carly

6.

Carly pulled her purple parka tighter as she waited by the curb. That was quite the wind out of the northeast. It whipped her hair, stung her eyes and chilled her to her core. Homeless people or pets left outside overnight would have a tough time. Snow flurries were expected.

But Carly felt warm enough, and totally pumped for her Certified Nursing Assistant exam. It was this very morning at the college in downtown Medford. Little Mike was with Sukaya, and Daddy Jack had promised her a ride on his way to work, albeit roundabout. Carly had no worries now but passing scores.

She was pretty sure she was prepared. Her on-site classes were long done, and she'd pulled an almost-all nighter now, studying and reviewing. So there was that.

Still, her stomach felt queasy. Nerves. She'd drunk way too much coffee to stay awake and cram.

I really should cut back. Look what it did to Nate.

He'd had far too much caffeine, what with super-sized coffees, sodas and those dumb energy drinks. When taken with too much alcohol, such trendy brews they could turn deadly. His being overweight hadn't helped.

When they were still together, Carly had driven Nate to the ER more than once. And then he'd driven her in his old beater, after he had an episode and pounded on her. He said she'd flirted with someone else. Which she would never do. So he'd blacked her eye, cut her lip. He was a big guy, and could have done a lot more.

Luckily there was only the one time. But that was enough. She'd seen what had happened with her birth mom, partly paralyzed and addicted to painkillers when a fight with Carly's step dad left her unable to work or even keep her kids.

Medics had patched Carly up, and she'd kicked Nate out for good despite his passionate promises to reform and find a job. She wondered now if he had done either. A mutual friend of theirs said he'd heard that after Nate's father died of alcoholism, the young man had joined a young-adult faith group and started helping the homeless, himself.

Right. And pigs can fly.

Carly looked up and down the street, and shifted from foot to foot in an effort to keep warm. Cars and trucks rolled by in a steady, if slow, stream. Brakes squealed, other people waited to cross at the far corner.

There came more tightening in her gut. Where the heck was Daddy Jack? He usually was so punctual. Was he okay? Maybe something had happened with Mama Ellen.

She glanced at her fogged-over Mickey Mouse watch. Fifteen minutes to eight. Jack was supposed to be here at seven-thirty.

Carly just couldn't be late for this test. If she were late, and failed to earn her caregiver's certificate, she'd have to wait months for another exam. Her piggy bank and savings account were down to a combined fifty bucks. She already had a tough time feeding herself and Mikey, never mind paying their rent. Hopefully the landlord would let her slide again.

No. Failing is absolutely not an option.

She would pass this test and take that job she'd tentatively agreed to, and a few more, pending her earning her degree. It was now or never.

Her fingertips began to numb, even in the mittens. Her eyes watered. Her ears tingled under the cap. She pulled her collar higher.

What had happened to Daddy Jack? She fumbled in her purse for her cell phone.

That's when she heard the blip of brakes on wet rubber, and the swoosh of tires sliding on damp pavement. Jack's pickup was taking the corner a bit wide onto her street. His pickup lurched to a stop, tailpipe spewing blue-white clouds of exhaust. The smell drifted over her.

Carly yanked open the door. She hauled herself up and in, not easy with her weight. She had vowed to cut back on snacks and macaroni once the pressure of the exam was coming off. But maybe not on designer coffee. It kept her going. She deserved at least one indulgence.

"Hey, Daddy Jack," she puffed, grinning at the man in the cap with earflaps that stuck out like dog ears. "I thought something happened to you or Mama Ellen. Can't be late for the test. Can you hurry?"

"Sorry I'm late, Carl, but you should be fine," Jack said, shifting into drive. He eased the truck back out onto the road. "We're only ten minutes away. Fifteen, at the most."

"Hope you're right. And thanks for the ride." She set her backpack on the floor.

"Anything for my baby girl. "You all ready for this test?"

"Ready as I'll ever be." She yanked out her seat belt, fumbled a minute, and snapped it. "Cold enough for you?"

"Oh yeah. Maybe a little too cold."

"What? For the Iron Man?"

"I didn't mean for me."

"Mama Ellen? Bet her arthritis is killing her." Carly rubbed her mittened hands to bring more feeling into them.

"Well, yeah. It's hard on Ellen. She said to tell you, 'hey.'"

"Hey. Bet she's been baking up a storm for Christmas, for church."

"The freezer's full. That tub next to me has cookies for you and Mikey."

"Thanks, Daddy Jack. We're down to our last two." She stuffed the small plastic container into a pocket of the backpack.

"Wish I could help. How's your little guy doing?"

"Pretty good. But then he's not. He kind of made sense the other day, and then had a setback. I can make more time for him after I get this test outta my hair."

While Jack drove the eight miles to Medford and the college branch where the tests were held, Carly listened to Jack tell her about the abandoned horse he'd taken to calling "Survivor." Told her all he knew or could find out about the ancient, hairy brown, sway-backed kindred soul of his up along the pass road laid over an ancient Indian trail.

Carole T. Beers

Carly had a hard time concentrating on Jack's tale, so worried was she about her test and being late. But she forced herself to listen, allowing some of his concern to seep into her bones. She'd always been able to feel what Jack felt, considering him practically flesh and blood.

"Did you check the Internet, Petfinder, anything like that?" she said.

"I did, a little," he said. "And the sheriff, of course. But I couldn't find anyone missing a horse. I'm beginning to think it was just turned loose to fend."

"That's so cruel. Like abandoning a child, almost. Someone who trusts you, relies on you for just about everything."

Carly heard her words as if they were coming from somebody else. Didn't Sukaya call that a Freudian slip? Where you said something that belied what you really thought but didn't dare say? Would she have to be give up on Mike, relinquish him to others' care, one day?

Daddy Jack hadn't noticed. "You got that right, Carl. And you or I could never do that, right? We're alike, that way. In a lotta ways." He chuckled. "Most of them good." He looked over at her and smiled.

She rubbed her arm, and returned his smile."Yes, you're right about that." Even so, she felt doubt creep in about never abandoning someone. She hoped he didn't notice.

"Hey! Here we are. It's eight straight up. Better get a move on, young lady."

"Yes, sir!" Carly unfastened her seatbelt, grabbed her pack and slid from the truck. Before closing the door, she added, "Did you put up a flyer for the horse at the farm store? Maybe The Expo? The fairgrounds where you took Mikey and me to a rodeo?"

"At the store. I might scribble something to put it up at the fairgrounds, but Central Point is pretty far from where the horse is. Hey, good luck on your test. Let us know."

"Will do. Hope they don't shut me out."

With that, she was gone, hurrying along the sidewalk and gently colliding with other late students pushing through the college building's glass doors.

Jack

7.

That night after work, which had taken him past the dinner hour, Jack split two logs and gathered up the kindling beside the porch. When he climbed back up to the house. His feet were half-frozen in the old brown slippers. His hands were practically frostbit. He hadn't taken time to don gloves.

It was pleasantly warm inside. Actually too warm. Green lay panting on the kitchen floor. But no matter how warm it might be, Ellen could still feel cold. So Jack tended the fire in the wood stove that provided their main heat before heading to the living room where the always-playing TV babbled in the corner.

He smelled fresh evergreen as he approached her recliner across from the Christmas tree. "How you doing, El? Warm enough?"

Ellen turned slightly in her chair so their eyes met. "Alive. Barely. But yes, warm enough, for once."

Her movement jostled Wilhelm, the three-legged longhair dachshund in her lap, but did not awaken him. She smiled enough to flash her dimples, and pulled the crocheted throw up to her chin. A mug and folded newspaper sat on the side table beside her. "How was your day?"

"Tolerable. I see you're watching 'Access Hollywood' Anything interesting?"

"Nah. The usual tramps and hunks pimping their projects. You're home kinda late." A statement, not a question, but one bearing a hint of criticism.

Jack's chest tightened. "Lots going on at work. Errands, and late traffic. There's a fire or something just down the block. Emergency vehicles. I had to wait awhile, then got rerouted."

"I heard the sirens, and wondered. The old Kretchmer farm? That junkyard and old barn just begging for the backhoe?"

"No. Farther down. That rundown ranch rambler. Tweakers. Probably cooking meth oil."

Green wobbled into the living room to stand facing Ellen, who reached over to ruffle the heeler's ears. Wilhelm snapped at the larger dog, who went to flop down near the Christmas tree.

Jack chuckled, and patted the weiner dog. "Hey, Willie." He looked his wife while he fondled the dog's ears. "You had dinner, El?"

"Spaghetti from last night. Heat some up for yourself. Oh, I made a pie."

His mouth watered. "What kind?"

"Apple. Grace next door still had some hanging on her tree, and brought them over. They were near the house where the deer couldn't get them."

"I'm surprised the apples weren't frostbit."

"They got lucky. Grew on branches under the eaves." She paused before turning back to the TV. "Know if Carly passed her test?"

"No idea. Don't expect she'd know this soon. But I'll call her later, see how she thinks she did."

"Bet she passed. She's a smart little whip."

Jack's stomach rumbled. He went back to the kitchen, and heated a plate of spaghetti. When it was steaming, he gingerly pulled it out and found a can of grated Parmesan in a cupboard.

He ate standing at the counter while Green sashayed and Wilhelm pranced around his ankles. Jack tossed each a noodle. Green's disappeared with a gulp, but Willy sucked it down slowly. Jack tossed two more noodles and watched the end of Willy's slap the dog's cheeks.

It reminded Jack of that silly, spaghetti-eating scene in the old Disney film, "Lady and the Tramp." One of his favorites, about a bad dog redeemed by love. He'd had to buy a second copy of the DVD after his foster kids watched it to death and then left it on the floor where Jack stepped on it. He wondered if Carla had shown Mickey the film.They didn't have streaming video then. Or if they did, he couldn't afford it.

Jack heaped a big slice on a small plate, reheated a mug of morning coffee, and returned to the living room. Sinking into the depths of his own recliner, he looked around at the wall of family photos. He wondered where some of their kids were this Christmas. He and Ellen had been unsuccessful in reaching all ten they'd taken in over the years. He hoped they weren't shivering under a freeway viaduct somewhere. He and Ellen's biological kids were busy with jobs and their own offspring in Seattle and Denver.

The weiner dog, not letting his three legs limit him, jumped back on Ellen's lap. But then, both his hind legs were intact.

"Find out anything about that old horse?" Ellen shouted above the TV noise.

Jack frowned. There was a whole lot of loud music, joking and laughter about celebrities Jack hadn't heard of and didn't give a rat's ass about. People famous for being famous, as the saying went.

Parasites. Lost to God, oblivious to all Creation.

"Made a flyer, and a few more calls," Jack said. "Don't think the old nag is gonna make it through the winter. Wish I could help."

"Any leads, at least?"

"Nope. Would you turn that TV down?"

A car-insurance commercial blasted from the TV speakers. Ellen pointed the remote as if it were a gun at the offending appliance, silencing it. Then she sat straighter, shook back her silver hair and nodded at Jack. "Hey."

"Hey, what?" he said, chewing pie while Green drooled on his slipper.

"I know you want to help, but we can't afford a horse. Your being laid off and all."

"Let's not get into that again, El." His stomach twisted as he recalled their argument of several nights ago. She'd made it clear they had no money to spare.

She raised her chin. "I saw on the news some big horse sanctuary in Ashland, is it Equamore or something like that? Needs donations and volunteers. They rescue horses in need. For life. And sometimes let people with special needs help out there."

Jack took a long swig of superheated coffee, and grimaced. It burned all the way down. But he heard his wife's words, and they'd clicked. "Huh."

"You should give them a call. They said a terminally ill girl was healed after interacting for a while with the horses."

Jack took another sip, this time more slowly. "Is that right?"

"Call them, Jack. Worth a try." She turned back to her show, reinstating the volume.

A sharp *pop!* sounded from the Christmas tree. The weiner dog sprang from Ellen's lap and broke into a barking streak before timidly investigating the fallen rocking-horse ornament.

Green, the more sanguine of the pair, merely flattened his ears.

Jack groaned and pushed himself up. He walked over to retrieve the plastic figurine. After retying it to the branch, he picked up his empty plate and went to the kitchen. There he found his phone, and Googled "horse rescue" and "Southern Oregon."

The word "Equamore" came up. He tapped the call icon.

The phone at the other end rang a long time. No one picked up. Of course. It was late.

Finally a recorded female voice expressed gratitude for the caller's interest in the Rogue Valley's leading equine rescue organization, politely asked for a donation no matter how small, and said to leave a message so the call could be returned.

Hope rising, Jack paused. Then he left his message. Told all about the old horse, how it had survived one winter, but might not survive a second. That it clearly had been of good and lengthy service to someone, but now was forced to fend for itself. In deep snow. During the Christmas season, at that, about which Jack said he felt particularly sad.

When he was ready to sign off, Jack thought of something else.

"I may be able to help a bit with the horse's up-keep," he whispered, so that Ellen would't hear—

something she seemed able to do even with a blaring TV. "I'm not a rich man, but I can help a little."

Jack felt he'd done all he could. It was now up to the Powers That Be.

He hoped the returned call would be in time. A sense of foreboding permeated him. That horse couldn't survive another winter.

It's exactly how Jack had felt last Christmas, before Ellen had the small stroke that ruined her balance, worsened her arthritis and essentially stole away the woman he'd loved. Anxious. Without his knowing what about.

It was also how Jack felt about Carly and Mike. Like something awful was about to happen, with him powerless to stop it.

Carly

8.

Carly hummed to herself as she tidied the kitchenette that afternoon. The window over the sink showed a crystalline world made bright by new snow, and brighter still by a weak sun. Excitement buzzed her as she thought of the lady she was going to help in the new job.

A puffy black-headed grey bird—what Suky called a junco?—hopped hopefully along the window ledge. It gave Carly a curious look.

"I'll leave you a dab of peanut butter when I get back," she said. It's what Daddy Jack used to do for hungry birds in winter.

The junco cocked its head and fluttered away.

It was a new day, Carly thought, even as her evening shift approached. And a new time for her and Mikey. She felt light, almost happy. She might stop by Past Perfect on her way there, see what new treasures had been donated. She could use some pajamas. Her white-flannel ones with fat, rolling ponies showed its years. Maybe she'd find something soft, pink and scented with fabric softener from the store's dryer.

The cuckoo clock read three-thirty. Time to get going. Another neighbor was waiting in his apartment to give Carly a ride. She only had to bundle up Mikey, drop him at Sukaya's inhome daycare center, and go. But when Carly looked over at the main living area, her heart plummeted.

Mikey hugged himself. He rolled over and over on the rug. He uttered clicking sounds. His rolling was gentle, the sounds, soft. But Carly felt a pain like a dull knife stab her gut.

"Honey. Mikey. Stop that." She had barely thirty minutes to get to work. This distraction would delay her. She couldn't afford to be late.

Mikey kept rolling back and forth. "Cookee, cookee."

"Not now, baby," Carly said, grabbling her purse and heading for the boy. She groaned in frustration when he pushed up and scooted beyond her grasp.

She relented, and went for the treat. The bribe would facilitate things.

One eye on the boy, Carly grabbed her two last cookies. She popped one into her mouth, savoring the cinnamon Mama Ellen had added to heighten the flavor of chocolate chips. Then, hurrying past the dining table, she slipped Mikey's pill bottle into her purse.

Mikey sat up, frowned and shook his head at the cookie offering. He stared at Carly as if she were a stranger.

No. Not another setback. Not with our future on the line.

Conscious of seconds ticking away like a time bomb, Carly swept the boy into her arms. She gathered her parka, along with the boy's Mikey's coat and cap, off a shelf by the door.

As she dressed him, she thought about how even her best efforts—thundershirts, massage, tough love— seemed to have failed to really ease his condition. The pills worked at first. Recently Mikey said some words that made sense. Murmured to pictures in his animal book. Acted like he might put on his own shoes. Even hugged her back.

Yet now he'd been clicking, rolling and resisting her. Pulling his arms away. Shaking his head. Devouring precious time and hope. He just could not focus on any one thing for long, except inappropriately or obsessively.

Carly felt as if she were sliding backward. Slipping down an icy slope. The abyss of despair, never far away even in the best of times, loomed ever larger.

Finished dressing the boy, she settled him on one of her ample hips. He went limp. She held him tightly. Shouldering her purse, she recalled the small victories.

I have to keep those in mind. Focus on when my efforts work. Build on the breakthroughs.

Those were times she let hope live in her heart, and entertained visions of a happy, normal life for them. Maybe even a life with a partner who could lighten their load.

But other times, like now, and even with the encouragement and help of friends like Sukaya and Jack, depression crept in and made itself at home.

She had to face it. There might never be a long-lasting improvement in Mikey's condition. Nothing like a normal life for them. Worse, she had to deal with it alone.

"Damn you, Nate!" she yelled, scaring off birds pecking on the iced-over porch. "Why'd you have to hit me? Go away? Your baby needs you. It would kill you to see him now."

A sob shook her, loosening her coat from her grasp. The parka crumpled to the floor in a purple heap. Mikey kicked free of her other arm and spun around on the threshold. She grabbed the doorframe for support.

"I just can't do this alone," she whimpered. "I need someone. Anyone. Or I have to...I have to find Mikey another home." She knew she didn't mean it. But the way things had been going, but it was a distinct possibility. If she had a breakdown, he would be taken away.

Her boy stared up at her, his pupils big, his mouth spilling saliva. Moments ticked away. Then he bolted into the darkening snowscape.

Jack

9.

Jack set down the phone. He stared out the kitchen window. Saturday. It was the third time in two days that he'd called the horse sanctuary, and still no call back. You'd think they would need all the volunteers and rescue opportunities they could get.

Annoyance coursed through him. His stomach churned.

That old horse might not make it through tonight's forecast blizzard up on the pass. He needed help now. What was Equamore's problem?

Jack finished the last bite of cold meatloaf sandwich, and sat for another minute. He bent to stroke Wilhelm, who trolled for tidbits anytime someone was in the kitchen. Green lay still at Jack's feet. He was secure in the knowledge he'd get treats whenever Jack indicated they were forthcoming. Jack obliged, giving him and Willy the few crumbs left on his plate.

He looked at his phone. It read one o'clock: getting late. He stood, and hollered into the living room. "I'm going out for a few hours, Ellen. Be back before dark." He hoped she hadn't heard because, if she asked, he couldn't tell his wife were he was going. They didn't need another fight.

The TV blared on without interruption. Ellen must be asleep. She'd been sleeping a lot more lately. Was her condition worsening?

On the chilly porch he set down his thermos and shrugged into his rubber boots, hat and fleece-lined jacket. After pulling on work-stained gloves, he retrieved his thermos. He took his time stepping down the slick steps to the carport and wrenched open the ice-stuck door of his truck. He let Green in first, and then hoisted himself onto the cold seat. Several stray snowflakes made their way onto the windshield, but melted when they hit the glass.

I'd better get a move on. Dark comes fast, especially before a storm.

It felt and even smelled like that predicted blizzard was not much more than an hour or two away. The wind had kicked up, ruffling fir branches along the driveway. A small pinecone fell, ricocheting like a bullet off the windshield.

When he got to the farm store fifteen minutes later, the parking lot bustled with shoppers laying in supplies: grain, shavings, wood pellets, batteries, kindling. They and their stock would be snug and safe while waiting out the storm.

Entering the store, Jack noted the row of snow shovels and blowers lining the wall outside the door. Sandbags stood beyond. De-Icer was prominently displayed just inside.

Red-cheeked men and women came and went, jostling for position at the cash registers, and pushing heavily laden carts outside.

Jack caught the eye of the cashier he'd seen a few days ago. The young man raised his eyebrows in acknowledgement, and then focused back on his customer.

It didn't take that long to stand in line to make his purchases. Jack stuffed the receipt for alfalfa hay and rolled barley into his jacket pocket, and climbed back in his truck to drive to the feed-and-bedding annex.

Soon a portly young man with a goatee and gold ear hoops was sliding two hay bales and a sack of barley into the bed of Jack's truck. Jack thanked him and drove off while the sky darkened and snow fell more steadily, making streets dicy to brake and stay straight on.

Packed snow was easy to drive over. But this new coating seemed as slick as deer guts on a doorknob. Jack grinned to himself as he found the turnoff to the old highway, and headed out of town.

"Slick as deer guts." He chuckled saying the phrase, and looked at Green, who cocked his head. It was an expression Jack heard a farmer use a long time ago, and then, as a hunter himself, appropriated as his own. You tended to collect unique expressions, working in the ag community. Farmers and ranchers shared similarities, such as a rightward alignment in politics. But taken as individuals they were as different as could be when it came to the comments and quirks.

Jack refused to focus on the fact he'd soon *not* be working. He'd face that when it came. Maybe they'd relent. It was hard to find good, seasoned help in the valley these days. Every no-talent with clean urine and a valid driver's license thought they were God's gift to an employer. But, Jack mused, even if hired, those culls wouldn't stay, ever hunting a larger paycheck for less work.

Traffic was light except for a smattering of trucks, four-wheeling hybrids and high-end SUVs. Jack drove cautiously but with urgency as the snowflakes fell faster, laying a thick blanket along the roadside. The warmer pavement melted the snow soon as it fell. But the feathery flakes showed an increasing inclination to stick.

Jack guessed the depth along the road at two inches and growing.

On the radio news show he heard a report that a four-wheel drive vehicle had run off the Greensprings highway. No injuries, thank the Lord. Not too far from where Jack was traveling.

He depressed the gas pedal. The truck groaned, then surged forward and settled into its task as the incline increased and the curves tightened.

In a half hour Jack drew closer to the spot where he always stopped to see the old horse, "Survivor," Jack felt excitement build. Hopefully the horse was there, and might understand Jack was there to help. This might be his last chance.

A broken-up hay bale, about a sixty-pounder, should keep the animal's belly full for a few days. These two bales might buy him a week.

Jack had learned from his ag clients that a horse in winter, depending on whether it is worked, needs two pounds of forage—either grass or hay—for each hundred pounds of body weight. More forage in winter. Jack guessed the weight of Survivor at about 800 pounds. So he would need at least 16 pounds a day.

When he came to the wide spot, he pulled the truck over and got out. He patted the cell phone in his coat pocket. He'd shoot photos of the horse to email to anyone who might know something about him, or want to help. These included a dozen clients over in Klamath.

He looked past the truck into the meadow. Falling snow dimmed the white landscape and dulled the black outlines of trees and brambles.

The old horse stood in profile only about a hundred-fifty feet from the road. He had his back to the wind rippling his mane and the base of his tail. When Jack got out of the truck and clomped around to drop the tailgate, the horse turned his wooly head to look. His ears pricked forward. Ghostly breath puffs encircled his face.

"Hey, boy," Jack called softly. "Brought you some dinner. Good stuff. Bet you haven't had a square meal in a long time."

One of the horse's ears flicked back, then swiveled forward again. His head lifted a few inches. His eyes brightened with curiosity.

Jack plunged a hay hook into one end of the bale, catching the iron point over tight baling twine, and dragged the rectangular block of fodder to the edge of the cargo box. He stuck the tip of the other hook into the bale's other end and dragged the hay out, taking most of its weight against his belly and thighs.

"Ooomph!" he said, rearing back, lifting the bale and laboring through thick snow to the meadow's edge. He was thinking he possibly could have driven the truck at least a short way onto the meadow. Maybe where the bank dropping into that meadow was less steep.

But Jack could not afford to take chances. He didn't want to get stuck. That would be a whole other nightmare.

Icy air stabbed at his throat as he crab-walked down the slope and across snow-mantled grass with the bale, slipping and sliding as he went. The snow was slick enough. The flat dead grass under it was slicker still.

He almost lost it more than once, swearing each time.

"Mother-effing ice," he spat one time. His other words suggested rude activities by anatomically incorrect creatures.

Momentarily relieved of his frustration, Jack began to chew on an idea. It probably would have been better to be out here on his old wooden snowshoes, if he'd thought of them earlier, and could've found them in that archeological dig he called a garage. If he came here again he'd wear them. They'd make the mission much easier.

Jack panted as he made his way with the bale, and sweated in his thick clothing. This was daunting work, much tougher than he'd figured. But still he inched along with the bale, moving ever closer to Survivor, stopping every few feet to show the old boy he meant no harm.

The animal stepped back. He lifted his head higher as Jack came, and shot rattling snorts and puffs of exhaled breath into the frosty air.

Suddenly Jack put a foot wrong. He knew it the minute he committed to the long step. Both feet slipped out from under him and he went down with the bale, dropping onto his left shoulder, swearing a blue streak. Snow filled his eyes and nostrils. He coughed and spat while brushing it off his face.

Then he heard the muffled staccato of galloping hoofs and felt the earth tremble. Ice pellets and wet snow peppered his face. He swiped at his mouth and eyes.

When he could see again, he saw that the horse had galloped away to who knew where, leaving behind churned holes in the snow. The smell of damp exposed earth filled Jack's nose. He sneezed, wiping his nostrils with his sleeve.

He pushed up and anxiously he scanned the meadow. Not a trace of the old horse. Just big hollow holes, giant blurred hoofprints, leading toward tall timber.

Well, what for-crying-out loud did I expect? That the horse would walk right up and personally thank me for the kindness?

This horse was now feral, he reasoned. Gone from tame to wild, and it had been that way a long time. Maybe it even was abused in its earlier life. Why should it trust humans again?

Jack actually knew little about horses, how or what they thought or felt. All he knew was, the animal better realize the bounty that had been dropped at his feet. Take advantage of it. Feed his pathetic starving skeleton, or he would surely die. Didn't need to be friendly. Just needed to stay alive.

The horse had to want that. Jack wanted that even more.

But Jack began to doubt it would ever happen. You could not *will* something to live, do a thing you wanted, be the way you needed it to be. That was just how things were.

Carly

10.

Carly flew out the door after Mikey. Heart hammering, she stared from side to side in the snowy front yard. She clomped around the side of the apartment building toward the alley.

No sign of Mikey, only the purple hollows of his footprints. He could be anywhere. Was he down at Suky's? In the alley with its weeds, beer bottles and garbage cans? She had no idea what would be going through his hazy, troubled mind.

Desperate, she went back around to the front and banged on Suky's door.

"Mikey's run away, and I can't find him!" she shouted at her startled-looking neighbor. Suky's two kids and a third one peeked wide-eyed from behind her. One sucked a lollipop.

"Haven't seen him," Suky said, blowing cigarette smoke out into the dim air. "Brrr! Get a coat on, girl, or you'll catch your death."

"No time. Gotta find Mikey." Her shouted words stung her aching throat.

Carly turned and lumbered toward the alley, slipping and sliding on uneven, uncertain ground. Mikey had been known to run that way before, to go through castoff boxes and other garbage. She once found him there gnawing a chicken drumstick.

"Mike," she now called. "Mikey! Where are you? Say something. Mikey!"

Carly listened hard, her heart beating like the pendulum of a runaway clock. The only sounds were of snow pelting a steel barrel on its side in the alley, and of cars passing on the snow-slick street at alley's end.

An odor of burnt leaves and woodsmoke hung in the air. The smoke stung her eyes and nose. She coughed, and spat to one side.

She walked through fresh snow closer to the alley and street. Nearby a small dog yapped. Maybe it was that scruffy mutt Mikey shared his drumstick with the time he was lost between trash cans.

What was that little brown dog's name? Scamper? Scooter?

"Mikey!" She yelled, hurrying on, her boots sliding with each step. At the end of the alley she looked around, feeling the cold more, growing her fear. There were the trash cans, all right, and there was the bright-eyed brown dog. It barked again and stood stiff-legged, its curled tail slowly waving.

Carly's muscles tensed. Adrenaline surged through her.

Is he going to attack? Can I escape through the neighbor's gate?

She had been used to the Penningtons' dogs when she lived there. But she never really warmed to them. When she was a toddler herself, a pit bull had bitten her hand after she'd offered it a treat. She liked animals all right, but never quite knew what they were thinking.

This dog now clearly didn't recognize Carly from that time she'd seen him with Mikey. Its hackles stood up.

She tried not to stare directly into its hard black-button eyes. She'd heard that kind of staring was a sure way to up a dog's aggression.

"Scooter," she said in an even but firm voice. "No!"

The barking stopped. The dog's head cocked to one side.

"Good boy," she said, breathless but wary. "Have you seen Mikey? You curled up with him once? The chicken bone?" She knew animals didn't understand human talk, but this one might sense her mission.

The dog briefly looked away, and then back at Carly. His eyes gave away nothing. But his tail waved more gently.

Carly continued on her desperate way, blowing snowflakes off her eyelashes, halting at the street's curb. She looked both ways. There were no vehicles or people in sight. The hushed blue landscape seemed alien, otherwordly. Snow continued to fall. She felt like were the last person on earth.

"Mikey! MIKEY!" she called into an impervious twilight.

The sound of an approaching vehicle made her look right. Twin headlights, slowly growing larger, threw an eerie spotlight on the scene.

Out of the corner of her eye she saw a small figure dash into the street thirty feet to her left. Her breath caught in her throat.

"No!" She yelled, waving her arms, looking from boy to car and back again. "Stop. Miiiikey!" Her words seemed to hang frozen in space.

She gestured, and screamed so hard she felt her throat would burst.

"No. NO-O-O!"

Still the car came.

A second later she launched herself into its path. The car's tires, no longer turning, made a loud shushing as the brakes were applied. Its headlights, dimmed by a curtain of snow, shone like flat haloed baseballs through the gloom. In slow-motion they grew even larger.

Time broke into freeze frames as Carly, blinded by the lights, churned toward her son who'd stopped in the center of the road to face the oncoming car.

"Mikey! No! RUN!" The words exploded from Carly's mouth, sending snowflakes swirling away like confetti.

The effort of her scream, her final dash over snow and ice, tore her feet out from under her. The landscape tilted sideways. Carly dropped onto one knee on the hard, slick pavement. She slid there, too, falling back and banging her head. Fiery pan shot up one leg. Light flared. Confusion bloomed.

What happened next was a blur. Lying flat, completely dazed, she saw a tall, skinny man in a Santa hat appear out of nowhere. He dropped the big sack he was carrying, and flew into the road. The onrushing headlights were only yards away.

Toddler and stranger melted together out in the street. The next instant, they stood on the far sidewalk.

Is this a dream? Or has Santa come to rescue my boy?

Shocked, and through a kind of veil, Carly saw the man kneel and embrace the boy before she uttered a deep groan and slipped into darkness.

Jack

11.

Jack half-ran, half stumbled to pick up his cell phone from the kitchen counter.

He didn't reach it in time. The call went to voice mail. He waited a moment, then dialed in the message. He put it on speaker mode so he could to be heard over the washing machine running through its spin cycle in the utility hall. Fixing that clunker would have to wait.

The voice message left by a man sounded high in tone and breathless, as if the caller had been running. Maybe was still running.

"Jack? Carly's foster dad? Nate. Found your number on her phone. She's been hurt. Call me ASAP."

Jack stared, uncomprehending, at the phone as the voice mail ended. It was as if he were trying to see into it.

Ellen's voice called out from the living room. She could be heard even over the washing machine, now winding down its cycle.

"Jack! Who was it? Carly's old boyfriend? What'd he want?"

"Not sure." He didn't want to upset his wife before he knew what was what. "I'm trying to call him back."

Breath coming in shallow draughts, Jack forced himself to stay steady as he hit the call button. Waiting for a pick up, he moved toward the living room and looked in. Ellen was down on all fours by the tree. She was sliding a white-wrapped gift box under the nearest branch. Wilhelm paced on three legs by her side.

"How'd you know it was Nate?" Jack asked.

His wife looked over her shoulder. "He called earlier but we got cut off. I couldn't return the call. Maybe he ran out of battery or service."

She straightened herself, reached out again, and then fell sideways. She caught herself by one hand on the arm of Jack's recliner.

"Ow! Dang! This new generic med is not helping my balance any. Not sure I can get up without help?"

"Coming, El." Jack started for the living room.

She struggled to rise, but fell back again. "I should keep trying to get up on my own. Doc says I have to do more for myself, work through pain. He says I need to move more, do things that are hard for me."

"Well, maybe he's right, El. What I've been saying all along."

Ellen swore mildly, but then chuckled and waved Jack away. She raised herself onto one knee, huffing and puffing to gain the other. Finally she stood. She gave Jack a thumbs-up, and hobbled back to her recliner.

He returned to the kitchen, tapped the callback number, and put the call on speaker mode.

Nate's tenor voice on the other end was saying something. Jack couldn't quite hear what.

"Sorry," Jack said. "Can you repeat that?"

"I said, 'Hey, Daddy Jack.' Isn't it what Carly calls you?"

"Did you say she got hurt? When? How bad?"

"She fell on the street trying to save Mike from getting hit by a car. As the Lord would have it, I was just passing by. I grabbed Mike just in the nick of in time. We're at the ER."

"She okay?"

"Got a sprained ankle, bad bruise on her knee and a concussion. But she and Mike are basically okay. She asked me to call."

Jack felt as if he'd hit an electric fence. "Wasn't she supposed to be at work?" He puzzled about that, as well as about Nate's "just passing by" claim.

"She had me call them, too," Nate said. "They were getting someone to fill in for her."

"But she's gonna be all right?"

"Yeah. It was weird, man, that I was there. Divinely inspired or something."

"So what were you really doing there, Nate?"

The breathing slowed on the other end. "I was on my way home from work, and I had something to drop off for little Mike." There was a pause. "And no, I wasn't stalking, if that's what you're thinking. I just wanted my boy to have a Christmas present."

"Okaaay." Jack waited to see if Nate would elaborate on his own.

You'd better be telling the truth, buster, or you're dead meat.

"I saw a kid run in front of a car, a woman chasing him. Didn't recognize them right away, but I managed to save the kid. I guess Carly fell."

A wave of weakness swept over Jack. He tried to put it all together. Believe Nate's story. He "just happened" to be in the area? His being there at the right time, bringing Mike a gift, might mean what it meant: a weird yet wonderful coincidence. But Jack felt uneasy. Had the young man heard Carly now had a job and was making money?

"Why didn't Carly call me?" Jack said. "And why was Mike running outside?"

"Docs are working on her, scans and stuff. Mike got out of the house, having an episode or something. Main thing, they're basically okay. Just glad I could help."

Jack's gut twisted. He knew Nate had thumped on Carly at least the one time. He worried that might be part of what had happened tonight.

One thing was clear. Carly was helpless. Jack needed to get to her. Now.

"It's been two years since you were in their life," he said. "Why would you suddenly decide to show up? She kicked you out, and you know why."

"Chill, man. Carly's OK with everything."

Being told to chill, and told by Carly's ex-flame, made Jack heat up. Made his heart beat even faster. "She never wanted to see you again. You should've called 911, let them handle it."

There was another pause. A cough at the other end.

"Hey. Jack. It was seriously a miracle I was there. It being Christmas, I wanted to give Mike something nice from the Co-op. I swear. I work there now. Saw you the other day but didn't say anything cuz I know how you feel about ... things."

Jack exhaled. "So it *was* you. You look different. Lost a lot of weight. But it still doesn't sit well, you're being involved here. About when did the accident happen?"

Jack wanted to recheck Nate's story for discrepancies. Being a father to all kinds of kids over the years had sensitized him to falsehoods and fabrications. He had a second sense about such things, and knew how to suss them out.

"Two hours ago. I called earlier and your wife answered but we got cut off. Probably the storm. Or my cheapo phone."

"I see." That sounded right. Jibed with what Ellen had said. "Well, tell Carly I'm coming, and will take them home. Get them settled."

Jack let out a breath. He rubbed the back of his neck. It was tight and sore, possibly from the call, or maybe from falling down on the mountain taking hay to Survivor.

Nate sounded as if he were telling the truth. Jack should give the kid the benefit of the doubt, be more charitable. After all it was nearly Christmas.

"Well, Nate, thanks for the call. I'm glad you were there. The Lord does sometimes work in mysterious ways."

"No problem. Hey. Merry Christmas, man."

"You, too, Nate. You too. Have a good one."

Ellen's voice cut in from the living room as Jack ended the call.

"Jack? Can you --? Oh, noooo!"

There came a loud swishing sound, a heavy thump, a glassy tinkle. Exactly the sound of a fully loaded Christmas tree hitting the floor. Wilhelm began to bark. Green raised up and walked toward the door.

Ellen called again in a higher voice. "I tripped over Wilhelm, that stupid dog. Now I'm down again and so's the tree. Hurry up!"

Jack rushed as fast as pain in his arthritic knees and hips allowed. Cold and stress could do that. First, Nate's disturbing call. Carly in jeopardy. Now Ellen's falling. Not to mention the predicament with the old horse. It was one crisis after another. Jack's usual philosophical calm was stretched to the breaking point.

He found his wife catawampus on their living-room rug. Wilhelm was licking her face.

"I'm here, Ellen. Don't move. Did you break anything?"

"No, no, don't think so. Willy, stop it!" She shoved away the dog. "What'd Nate say?"

"Hold on, El. Let's get you up."

Jack lowered himself onto his knees, worked his forearms under Ellen's torso and began to lever her up while Willy now licked *his* face. The effort to lift his wife took all his strength.

El weighs way more than a bale of hay, he thought, faintly amused at the comparison.

Jack managed to sit her leaning against his chest, and then pull and lift her to her feet. Holding her around the waist and shoulders, he walked her toward her recliner.

"Ooof!" she said, dropping into its brown-leather depths. "I'm sore, but okay. I think. I'm anxious to hear what Nate said. Was it about Carly? If he hurt her, I'll strangle him with my own two hands."

Jack searched Ellen's worried eyes.

"Carly sprained her ankle and got a concussion, falling on the street," he said. "Chasing Mike, who somehow got out of the apartment and ran onto the road. They're basically okay, though. They're over at the hospital ER. I'm gonna go there now, you don't need me."

Ellen's eyes looked childlike in their fear and worry. "Just tell me what happened. I can deal with the truth, but not with lies or uncertainty."

"Nate apparently was going over there with a Christmas gift for Mike when he saw a woman chasing a kid, with a car coming. She fell, but Nate saved Mike from being hit."

"What? That's a crazy story. But glad they're OK."

"You and me, both."

"I hate that Nate was in the area, even with a gift." She sighed. "But, I guess we have to hope he's telling the truth."

"No choice."

Ellen pursed her lips, still stained a soft pink from her morning makeup routine. "What do you make of the story?"

"Again, trying not to think the worst, it being Christmas. I guess it was him I saw working at the farm co-op last week. He's more mellow, lost a ton of weight. Now he wears a cross around his neck instead of a skull."

Ellen pulled her afghan over her legs. Wilhelm jumped up to curl in her lap."Did you talk to Carly?"

"They're still working on her. I'll just go on over there, and wait until I can drive her and Mike home."

Ellen nodded, her eyes full of concern. "You be careful, Jack. Such terrible weather." She twisted the edge of the afghan. "I need my meds. Would you bring them?"

Jack looked at her more closely. There was a softness about her tonight, a vulnerability she didn't often let him see. The fall, the worry about Carly and Mike, seemed to have melted Ellen a bit. Melted him some, too.

"Now don't you worry, El. Relax. Maybe I should take you to the ER to get checked out, too. Sure you're okay?"

"I'll live."

Jack ran his hand over her silver hair, surprised by its luster and softness. It rarely saw a hairdresser, or hair product of the expensive kind. Yet it fell in thick waves over her round shoulders, and curled out saucily at the bottom.

He turned and walked to the bathroom. He found what she needed among the grouped vials and bottles, and came back with the right pill along with a glass of water.

"Thanks, hon," she said, looking earnestly into his eyes. "What would I ever do without my Jack?"

The hint of a dimple played around her smile. Jack glimpsed for a moment the girl he'd married. Then that girl's face dissolved back into Ellen's puffy, tired one.

Jack fumbled for her hand, raised it to his lips and kissed it.

Her hand, small in his, felt like satin and smelled of rosewater.

Carly

12.

Carly opened her eyes. She felt sleepy. Her eyelids seemed sticky, as if she'd cried. She saw the living room in a blur, but then found her focus on the dome light.

She lay blanketed, on her back, in her sofa bed. Her head swam from, what? Medication? She didn't recall having taken any. She must have nodded off. Where was Mikey?

Oh, right. I'm hurt.

It slowly came back to her, and it didn't please her. She'd fallen while chasing Mikey on the snowy street. The same snowy street where the boy was saved from being hit by a car. Saved by...Nate. Supposedly bringing Mikey a present. Right.

And she was the queen of Romania.

She'd asked Nate so many questions on their ride to the ER, then again while waiting for treatment under the stark lights of the green rooms with piped-in holiday Muzak. She couldn't remember all his answers, but they hadn't raised red flags.

The leg throbbed now. But, thanks to the meds they'd given her, that pain was dull and bearable. Her ankle felt stiff, as if in a brace. She tried to move it under the covers, but ceased when it didn't respond.

"Ay," she said to herself. "I got it. Sprained ankle, slight concussion. Daddy Jack brought me home from the ER. Mikey? You here?"

Her breath felt thick in her throat. She turned her gaze to the room.

Little Mike lay on his stomach on a strange, fluffy brown something—a wadded blanket?—surrounded by shredded wrappings in front of the Christmas tree. The boy stared at the TV by the tree. Its images bounced with some kids' musical show starring crayon-colored unicorns.

Carly let her eyelids fall shut. It felt so good just to drift.

Almost as quickly she opened her eyes again and stared at Mikey. She knew what the boy Mikey was lying on. But she didn't remember buying any stuffed animal. One that resembled, what? A curled-up brown pony with shiny chocolate eyes? But the animal was there, Mike nestled in its plump embrace.

It slowly came back to her. This must the present Nate claimed he'd brought for Mikey.

What she thought next piqued her curiosity. Really? Was simple gift-bearing really behind Nate's stated reason for being in their neighborhood? She ached to find out.

Nate had left the ER a little before Daddy Jack arrived. Left the wrapped present, too. They'd made her stay the night at the hospital since she had a concussion. Daddy Jack had driven her and Mikey home early this morning, and settled Carly in with blankets and water.

Oh, yeah. She was supposed to call if she needed help. Daddy'd be back in a flash.

That was the last thing she'd remembered. Now a glance at the cuckoo clock over the TV told her it was past noon. *Uh-oh.* She had to be at work at four. But how could she? Certainly not with a badly sprained ankle. Not to mention, a concussion.

She had to call to let them know her predicament. Then she remembered Daddy Jack saying he'd called the lady she was scheduled to work for last night. Carly's brain was toast.

What a mess? Why me? And why at Christmas, when I have so much to do?

Her stomach grumbled. She had been knocked out for a pretty long time.

"Mikey?" she said, looking over at him on the rug. "You OK? Want something to eat?"

The boy, lying with his stuffed horse, raised his head. "Where Daddy?"

"Daddy Jack?" She was happy to hear his words, a sentence. "You want Daddy Jack?"

Mikey turned his attention back to the pony rug. He began to stroke it. "No," he said, looking confused.

He's not the only one.

Carly decided she should try to get up and find them something to eat and drink. But as she considered how best to raise herself, turning the crutch against the sofa to a useful position, she again thought of Nate. Or a man calling himself Nate. The man who'd saved Mikey looked like Nate in the tats, in the hair and eyes, and he sounded like Nate. But this man was skinnier, much nicer, and regarded her with a gaze more knowing than the last time she'd seen him.

It certainly was not the Nate she had known, and hoped to marry two years ago. She remembered having said as much last night as he'd driven her and Mikey to the ER.

"I can't believe you're the same man…OW!" she said, trying to blot out a throbbing pain in her ankle and knee. "Maybe his brother, but definitely not Mikey's father." She glanced over her shoulder to check on the boy, wrapped in a blanket in his carseat. "You're so different."

"Made some changes," Nate said with a nod and a hint of the goofy grin she once loved. He pulled a cross on a cord out from inside the neck of his hoody.

She pointedly looked at the cross. She also noticed a red-and-white Santa hat on the car's dash. Her supposed hallucination, that Santa had saved her son, had been no dream.

Another pain shot up her leg. Carly groaned, and shifted position in the seat so her ankle was raised a little. "God, this hurts!"

"Hang on, Carly. Almost to the ER."

"You better be telling me the truth. Don't get any ideas, though. What's done is done."

"Hey. I get it."

A few minutes passed with no talking as she tried to ignore the raging ache in her leg "Thanks for saving Mikey, and driving us to the ER."

"No problem. Glad to help."

"Can you hurry? This leg is killing me."

"I'm on it." Nate pushed the car forward, barely making it through he next light before it turned red.

Carly gulped. "You should've just called 9-1-1. You know you can't be in our life."

"After this you won't see me again. Promise." Nate set his jaw and looked straight ahead.

Huh, she thought now, sitting up in her sofa bed. Was this Nate legit, bringing the present, saving her and Mikey? The old Nate always had an angle, was always two steps ahead. If she saw him again she'd observe every gesture, listen for what was behind each word. Maybe he'd heard Carly was working now, bringing in money.

Her caregiver jobs. Carly's heart thumped at the thought of them. How could she work, in the shape she was in? She was the one who needed caregiving. She was the one needing money, more than welfare or social security brought in.

She also wondered how long she'd be laid up. Some people with sprained ankles could walk with the right brace in a week or so. But could she help disabled people walk? Or drive to appointments? Shop and fix meals? Let alone haul them on and off beds and toilets.

Sick with worry, she managed to push herself off the sofa bed, straighten the crutches to where she wanted them and hobble over to the kitchenette. There she brewed coffee and poured milk for her and Mikey.

Feeling a little better now that she had a purpose, she rustled about for an English muffin to toast, found peanut butter and picked up her cell phone to call Daddy Jack.

"Carly?" he shouted. It sounded as if he were driving. "You OK? How's our Mike? Need anything?"

"We're fine. Kinda. Not in need yet, but I may be soon," she said. She shared her worry about her jobs. "Thanks for bringing me home. I'll call if anything changes or I need help."

"You do that, Carl. Put me on speed dial. Can I call your clients or the agency?"

"I can handle it. Don't know how we'll get by. I guess it'll be day to day."

"Well, you know I'm here to help. Drive you, whatever. Let me know. Mama Ellen says hi. Get well soon."

"Tell her 'hi,' back. Love you guys."

"Will do. Right back atcha, Carl."

The cell phone perched on her shoulder, Carly took a sippy mug of milk in to Mikey. He took the mug and drank a little. Then he lowered the mug and held it to the face of his plushy horse.

Carly was spellbound a moment. But Daddy Jack was saying something. "You haven't heard any more from Nate, have you?"

"Oh, no. Thank goodness. He promised to stay out of our life. I believe him."

"Well, that's a blessing. Hey, you take care, Carl."

"Will do. You too."

After she hung up, she called her client and the agency. Those Daddy Jack hadn't called expressed shock when they heard what had happened, but assured Carly they'd find substitutes until the day when she could return to work. Which she said might be a week, but likely a little more. A tiny falsehood. She was determined to heal fast. Daddy Jack could drive her places, at least for a while.

Bracing one crutch against the sofa bed, she unstuck Mikey from his new friend, dealt with an almost-tantrum, and nudged him to his high chair at the table. She settled him there, smeared toasted muffins with PB and J, poured a cup of dark coffee with caramel creamer, and eased herself into a chair across from him.

Carly watched Mikey stuff his breakfast into his mouth and, in the process, smear some of it on both hands, his hair and the table. He looked so doggone helpless, so adorable and goofy, she felt her heart swell with love.

Those dimpled knuckles! How had she ever thought she couldn't care for the boy? This was her boy, her own flesh and blood, her opportunity to make things right for herself. She couldn't love him any more. She had to make things work for them, no matter what.

Cleaning up after breakfast, she hoped this medical absence wouldn't go against her. There was little help for it. She just prayed it wouldn't turn into a big problem.

Her thoughts drifted back to Nate. Her heart jumped a little. He'd looked so good now. She wondered again if his so-called changes were real. And if they would last.

She forced herself to think of other things. Like the gifts she hoped to give Mikey, and buy for a few select other people for Christmas. Visions of toys, and kitchen utensils, and wonderful new clothes filled her mind.

They were an effective distraction. It wouldn't do to get her hopes up about Nate. She had been burned before, and badly.

Jack

13.

From work, Jack made another phone check on Ellen, who was back to round-the-clock cooking for the church's bake sale. Waiting for her to answer, he looked around the back office he shared with two other salesmen. He kept his fingers busy flipping a logo pen, and his eyes occupied staring at an Old West calendar, his computer monitor decorated with notes, and a gilded toy-tractor they'd given him on his 25th workaversary. It was remarkably detailed.

"Hey," said Ellen's voice in his ear. Her TV was burbling in the far background, so she must be in the kitchen.

"You all right, El?"

"Depends what you mean by 'all right.' Heh, heh."

"I'm headed home, but might take a while. Got some late business."

She said she'd taken to using the walker on-wheels-and-tennis balls he'd rigged up after her recent fall. The newer meds affected her balance, so a lower dosage might be in order.

Satisfied with the information, Jack hung up, pulled on his coat and hat, and turned out the office lights. When he closed the door, he felt a pang of sadness. He'd sure miss this place. What did he have? Another week? Ten days?

His cell phone rang as he neared the front doors. It was the usual sound of a bugling elk. He always got a kick out of that. Plus it brought curious stares from uninitiated onlookers. Of course today there were none, not at six o'clock in an echoing ag supply house on a snowy Thursday evening.

The ID pane read, "Equator."

Finally.

He leaned against the door jamb, a wisp of hope rising in him. If he'd had a cigarette, he would have lit it and taken a long, celebratory draw. Savored the slow-building euphoria. But since he'd kicked the habit last year after coughing up blood during a bout of bronchitis, smoking was not an option. He still missed it, though.

The number on the call was unfamiliar, but had a local prefix.

"Hello?" said a female voice.

It was somewhat familiar, but not one he immediately recognized.

"Jack Pennington?"

"One and the same."

"Janine Bartell here, with Equator? You called and left a message a few days ago about an old horse you saw up on the Greensprings?"

Jack straightened and and peered through the sliding glass doors, where he saw snow falling again. The cab of his truck at the end of the lot sported a snow beret.

"Yes," he said. "I'm so worried about the old guy. I wondered if you or one of your people could go up there, and see if he might be a candidate for rescue?"

There came a pause. A shuffling of papers, or what sounded like it.

"It is so good of you, Mr. Pennington --"

"Jack."

"Jack, then. So good that our neighbors like you are keeping an eye out for animals in need. Thank you for thinking of us."

"Yeah." He pushed on. "I took some hay up there a while ago, to get him by until you could go up. But there's even worse weather forecast, so the sooner we could go, the better."

"First of all, Jack—and again, thank you for your concern. First and foremost, as you doubtless know, we are a dedicated rescue facility, and very committed to our mission. We couldn't exist without caring people like you, and without your generous donations."

"Of course." Jack sensed this call might not go the way he expected. He began to pick at a hangnail.

"Second, Jack, I must apologize for not getting right back to you. We had an emergency here at the facility, one that required my full attention. Sadly, we are not always as fully staffed as we would like. Volunteers sometimes have other priorities, and we rely heavily on our volunteers ..."

Her voice droned on. It was a bright, intelligent voice, but one given to too many words at a time when Jack needed just a few: "We will help."

"Yes," he said. "I do understand. I'm sure you run a taut ship, always needing money and people. As I said, I can offer some compensation for you to take this old guy. I think he's got a ton of heart, and put in his time for someone. It's really unkind that he's been put out to pasture this way. Just left to his fate."

"Third," said the woman. "And yes, I do hear you. And agree with you. Many horses have that happen to them. That's part of the reason Equamore exists. But again, we have very limited space and even fewer resources to support another horse, particularly an old one that brings with him all the problems associated with age. Teeth, hooves, joints, gut. Keeping an old-ster, especially one that's not been kept up, gets really expensive in a hurry."

"But," Jack said, balling one hand into a fist and then unballing it. "Okay. I understand. But you should at least have someone look at this horse. I would pay for the gas and time, if someone would go look at him. I'll send photos so you can see that a great guy he is."

There was a long silence. The sound of whinnying and stamping horses could be heard in the background. She must be in or near the stable. A warm, dry stable. A stable with plenty of fresh clean water, and well-cured, nutritious hay. A place were Survivor could live out his last days in good health and relative happiness, with other horses, and caring humans, all around.

"You are determined to help him, I see that," said the woman. "So I feel you possibly would play an important role in his maintenance."

"I said I would," whispered Jack, feeling hopeful once more.

"All right. But we can't send someone up, or I could not go myself, at least until I get through the next two or three days. That's the best I can promise, for now."

Relief flooded Jack. Something might be done. He knew if she only could see the horse, appreciate his stoicism and stamina despite his age, she would be hooked.

"Thank you. Right. Shall I come over to the facility and lead you up there?"

"That sounds good, Jack. Saturday, about ten, after we feed and water for the morning?"

"And maybe we could bring a halter and rope, and a trailer, just in case? Some hay and grain to lure him in? I have a truck. He's pretty skittish, but maybe—"

"Let's not hope for too much, Jack. Tell you what. I will make some calls first, see if we can track down an owner. Perhaps we can shame them into taking the horse back, or help them buy hay, if that was the issue. Give me a few days."

Jack slumped, and leaned his shoulder against the door frame. "Oh. Sure. I just thought..."

"I am not saying we won't go up and take a look. But I can't promise anything. As I saw, we really have no room for another horse."

"And as I say, I can help. I mean it. If you can't locate the owner, of course. Not sure he will make it through this coming storm." Jack bit off the hangnail he'd been worrying. His stomach was in a knot.

There was a brief pause. In the background of the other end of the line, a dog yipped and a child laughed. A rolling, bubbling laugh. A volunteer at the rescue? The lady's grandson?

"All right," she continued. "I hear your concern. Let's say if I cannot find the owners in the next day or two, I will go up with you and take a look. Or try to. How's that?"

Jack

14.

Jack could barely get through the next days and nights. He couldn't sleep. He had trouble concentrating at work. He lost his truck keys twice, once at home to Wilhelm, who snagged them off the coffee table and carried them outside, likely to bury them. And once in the toilet bowl.

The last straw, Jack forgot to bring home the canned milk and three dozen eggs Ellen had requested for her baking project, which culminated in the church bake sale the Sunday before Christmas. Ellen had not been a happy camper, and Jack made suitable apologies.

Every time the phone rang at work, Jack jumped, hoping it was the Equamore lady with news that the horse's owner had been found. But every time he answered, it was a sales call, a complaint or a wrong number. Or else Carly needing a ride to a client's home the next day, and some housekeeping help, which Jack never begrudged her. In fact, tending to such things kept him busy, as business at the ag supply house were beginning to slow for the holiday season.

A big blizzard swept in the night before the hoped-for horse rescue. A full foot of fresh, wet snow got dumped over the town and surrounding countryside. It brought with it winds that howled down chimneys and shook the bones of houses.

Jack stayed up late one night running to the nearby mini-mart for more milk and eggs for Ellen, paying way too much for them, and then hunkering down in the living room while Ellen took turns baking and napping. That night she was baking extra gingerbread men for Carly and Mike.

About midnight, Jack got up from bed and paced in his worn corduroy slippers through the house, and to and from the porch, keeping the fire stoked and the chill at bay. He ate a cold leftover burger without a bun. Catsup, pickle slices and extra salt made it slightly palatable.

Finally, unable to relax, Jack went out to the icy garage with Green hard by his heels. He pulled aside boxes and tools, sacks of this and that, shovels, and cans of screws and nails. When dislodged oddments dropped from the wall or sprang from shelves, he dodged or caught them. He skinned more than one knuckle, successfully cracked his shins on the workbench, and spat cobwebs and curses.

At such times, when he unleashed a torrent of verbal venom, he felt better. It cleared brain and body to curse a little, where no one heard except the heeler, who was used to it.

Green dogged his every step. He seemed to feel the anxiety his owner felt, but wrinkled his forehead as to what it was all about.

Jack gave him a reassuring pat. He once flipped the dog over on the mat and gave him a good belly rub.

At last Jack found what he sought. He loaded the scuffed, clunky wooden snowshoes into his truck.

Then he went inside and fell into bed, clothes and all, and enjoyed a short sleep.

The big day dawned at last. If you could call a flat grey punctuated with eye-searing white, proper "dawn." Jack had to clear the back steps and shovel a narrow path to his truck before he set out. Sweat coursed down his chest and back.

Finished, all ready to go, and standing in the kitchen filling his thermos with coffee, he looked at his phone. He was almost afraid to call Equamore to see if the "look-see" still was on. But he called anyway.

"I am so glad you called, Jack," said Janine Bartell. "We are super busy. Somewhat like the U.S. Postal Service. On the job no matter what the weather. But I made a promise, and I will try my best to keep it."

"Great. Shall I come over right away?"

There was a pause. Again the sound of rattling paper. A throat clearing.

"Well, that's what I needed to talk with you today, Jack. I have made some calls regarding the horse, but haven't narrowed it down to a possible owner or owners. And something has come up, so I really haven't enough time today to go up there. We maybe could try to look at your horse next week."

Jack's spirits plummeted. It was like a black cloud had come down on his heart. He resolved to stay positive, sound upbeat. But it wasn't easy.

"Look, ma'am. I took him hay last week. But it's likely long gone, by now. After this big storm moves through the snow may be too deep and heavy for him to forage." Jack left off to give her time to contemplate the consequences.

Another silence, again too long. Was she backing out of the whole deal? Or had she ever really intended to go up there in the first place?

Jack let out a sigh. He intended for her to hear it, and the desperation behind it.

"OK, Jack. Tell you what. If you are going up there anyway today, why don't you take and send some photos? And I can call the farm store, to let you draw on our account for another bale of hay to get the old guy through. Fifteen or twenty dollars' credit."

"Sure. Sounds good."

But Jack was fighting mad. His temples pounded. The woman had broken her promise to go look at the horse, possibly rescue him this very day. What could be more demanding of her time than a rescue? Wasn't that her business?

He knew he had no choice. He had to do what she suggested. And pray he could get up there, that the hay would see the old horse through the blizzard.

When Jack hung up, he peeked into the bedroom where Ellen still slept. He touched her shoulder, saw her open her eyes, and said Equamor was giving him credit for a bale of hay, and he was going to pick up the feed and drive it out to the horse. Yes, he'd be careful.

His drive up the Greensprings took longer than Jack expected. The bright white landscape nearly blinded him. And he was dead tired. Occasionally looking over at Green relieved his eyes.

It had not helped that Jack also had driven to driven Carly to her caregiver's jobs the past week, helped her do some chores for clients, and tried to keep his own boss placated—although that boss was no stranger to Jack's occasional absences to administer acts of charity over the years. One act had helped the boss's teenage son sidelined by a bull-riding accident. The boy needed trips for therapy appointments over months, and Jack had obliged when he could.

Now, in this whiteout morning in the middle of nowhere, Jack turned his mind to the task ahead. Called on his soldier-like discipline.

He found the wide spot on the snow-blanketed road. He edged over and took a bracing swallow of thermos coffee. Then he got out and strapped on his snowshoes. Not so easy, as the straps were stiff from neglect. It didn't help that his fingers were freezing.

At last, and with care, he got the showshoes snugged on his boots. He took their measure, rocking his feet back and forth and front to back to refamiliarize himself with their feel. It must have been ten years since he'd used them on an outing with Ellen and the kids.

Holding his arms out for balance, Jack walked a few steps. He set each showshoe down carefully. He wiggled them each time to secure their footprint and then moved at an inchworm pace across a crusted mantle of snow.

Satisfied he could do this, he blew snowflakes off his eyelashes and walked like a moon astronaut to the truck cargo box.

It stopped snowing. It even began to look like a weak sun might come out.

Hope and coffee warming him, he scanned the vast meadow. Its crisp, clean smell and stillness were overpowering but pleasant. Not one bird called, not one twig cracked, not one vehicle passed on the road to shatter the calm.

Jack's heart beat with excitement when he spotted the old horse, tucked in once more behind brambles. Branches and dead leaves covered with snow partially curtained the equine from view.

The horse raised his head at the sound of the truck tailgate dropping.

Jack paused to make sure the horse hadn't panicked at the rusty metal sound. It had not. But its head was even higher.

Bending forward, Jack double-hooked one alfalfa bale, pulled it off the truck and braced it against his hips and thighs.

"Here goes nothing," he said, canted to one side, hooked into the bale and moving one slow shoeshoe at a time. He took it easy, trying to take some pleasure in the slog. It was hard, sweat-provoking work.

But it's for a great cause: Life.

Besides, he and Survivor had kind of become brothers. Both were wracked by age. Not always understood or cared for. No longer handsome. But tough, through and through. Storm-weathered. True warriors.

As if in answer, as if in support, the sun did appear, ghostlike, through the white gloom. Jack thought he might even be able to snap a few good photos.

He made slow progress, crunching painstakingly with the hay bale toward the bank and slope leading down to the meadow. Sometimes his snowshoes sank deep in invisible soft spots, nearly disappearing. Other times they slipped on the icy crust.

Jack wished he'd had ski poles to brace himself. But keeping a lower center of gravity, the bale banging hard and heavy against his legs, he inched into the meadow.

The mission at least twenty minutes because he had to set down the bale from time to time. He was a sweaty mess when he reached the bramble and dropped the hay. A quick slice with his pocket knife freed the bale from its twine.

Jack balled up the twine, stuck the wad in his back pocket, removed his gloves and took out his cell phone. He put it in camera mode, looked up and gave a low whistle.

"Come on, now, Survivor. Old man. I know you're in there. Brought ya dinner again. Things will get better if you just hang in a little bit longer."

The thought surfaced that this was advice Jack could well take, himself.

He shot a few photos of the horse from forty feet away, as it puffed out steamy breaths and stared warily in his direction. He walked farther down the bramble, toward its end, and clicked more pictures. He even took a short video.

The sky darkened again. A few tentative snowflakes floated down. Jack became aware his feet and hands were nearly frostbit. His nose dripped onto his hand. He put away the phone.

Snowflakes fell more swiftly now, coating Jack's lashes. The wind rose, roaring in his ears. The bramble's branches whipped like angry snakes.

It was time for Jack to skedaddle. What happened next was up to the horse. And Providence.

Jack

15.

Early Sunday morning Jack was emailing photos of Survivor to Equamore when his wife talked him into going to church. He really didn't want to, but had promised Ellen many a time that he would. She reminded him this was the last Sunday before Christmas. How could he argue? Besides, she needed help taking her pies, cakes and cookies for the sale afterward.

Though he didn't want to go, and the drive was slow through new snow to reach their worship center, with more snow threatening, church was as good a place to be as any. It kept Jack's mind off Ellen's troubles, Carly's problems with the hurt leg and Nate, and on old Survivor, who might not live up to his nickname after all. Also off Mike, facing his own dim prospects.

In church they saw friends, sang carols, heard a retelling of the Christmas story from the Book of Luke and lit candles at the front of the poinsettia-bedecked sanctuary.

At the start of the service, the chapel felt cold and the congregation not much warmer. But with the arrival of a handful of scrubbed, bright-eyed youngsters to hear the children's sermon, the atmosphere in the sanctuary warmed up.

Sanctuary. Isn't that what some called animal-rescue outfits? They should rescue me.

People shared stories of blessings, and joined in prayers for the hurting. Jack's troubles seemed puny compared to those of people who faced cancer or lost loved ones. It was hard to stay worried or cynical. His expression changed, and he put extra effort into singing "O Little Town of Bethlehem."

The glow stayed with Jack the rest of the day. Even during that 90-minute bake sale in the overheated social hall, noisy as it was with people crowding each other and engaging in chit chat. That was partly because every one of Ellen's baked goods was snapped up, at a good price, with proceeds going to the church and its homeless-people assistance program.

In the end Jack was glad he'd gone, and told Ellen so when he helped her up the snowy back steps at home. She'd left the walker there; she didn't like to be seen with it in public. Besides, she was trying to do more by herself.

"Nice service," Jack said, shepherding her into the kitchen. "Good stuff to think about."

"Really?" Ellen brightened, took his hand and kissed him with feeling.

He felt a blush creep up to his cheeks and ears. He went ahead and kissed her back, a good long one. Then he had another cup of coffee and a Russian teacake, tossing a few tiny crumbs to Wilhelm and Green.

In the evening as Jack and Ellen watched the news on TV, they sat at attention when the anchor segued from reports of homeless counts to the story of a Sheriff's Department seizure of animals from a hoarder outside of town. The reporter stood in front of a ramshackle farm with pallets and baling-twine fencing.

Then he backed away to reveal a corral full of bony, hairy horses standing knee-deep in muck.

The reporter said at least one horse would be euthanized, so severe were its health issues. One mare had aborted her foal.

After the report, Jack sat for one long moment with his eyes closed.

"Damnit!" he suddenly shouted, rising from his chair. His empty mug thumped to the rug.

"Jack!" said Ellen, concern etching her face. "It's awful. But you can't take it personally. You can't save the world."

He stooped to retrieve the mug, grimacing as he felt a stitch in his back. "Maybe not. But I can sure as hell save one horse at a time." Still feeling pain, probably from having taken the baled hay to Survivor, he snatched his cell phone from the side table. He stabbed the numbers. His hands trembled, and a chill shook his bones.

There was no answer on the other end. But there was a voice mailbox. His face shading to crimson, he spat his words into the phone.

"Miz Bartell, or whoever answers the call on behalf of Equamore. This is Jack Pennington. The man you told you a good horse needs saving?" He paused, considering his words, and then decided to just let fly. "You've put me off for weeks with one excuse or another. Say you will, say you won't. I think you, by God, owe it to your supporters, to me, and to that old horse out there on the Greensprings, to take action. And take it now!"

He paused again, hearing a slight echo of his words. Green gave him a worried look.

When the recording asked if Jack were satisfied with his message, or had any more to say, Jack knew he'd said what he'd meant, no more, no less. He clicked off the phone and slammed it down. Spittle coated his lips.

Ellen stared at him in disbelief. But wisely, she said nothing.

An hour later, when he was in the bathroom getting ready for bed, the phone rang from its perch on the sink counter. The ID pane showed "Equamore."

Jack felt a jolt of fear in his chest Maybe he shouldn't have let his anger get the best of him during that call. Now he'd made an enemy, tarnished his soul and probably wrecked Survivor's chances of being rescued.

Well, it is what it is. And I'm not a bit sorry.

He let the phone ring a few more times, composed himself, and picked up the call.

It only took a few minutes. Afterward, he slept better than he'd slept in weeks.

Jack

16.

As Jack drove his truck down the farm-lined road east of the I-5 freeway, his heart raced with excitement. He felt like a kid again, a kid anticipating Christmas morning. And it was practically Christmas. Two days away.

He hoped he would have the present he wanted more than anything on Earth: the rescue of Survivor.

Nothing was certain, of course. Janine Bartell had made that clear, both earlier and again on the phone last night. She'd warned Jack not to count on a positive outcome, a forever rescue or adoption.

But she had called him back. So still Jack hoped.

He slowed the truck to a crawl. He'd been reading mailbox numbers for a mile. Each time he saw a big barn or stable he'd slowed even more, eliciting the occasional car horn toot or horn bray from vehicles behind him on the old highway.

Jack understood the drivers' impatience. Christmas was near, and these were the last few days for people to get out and get their trees or gifts. Time was a-wasting, and tempers were flaring. Holiday hares didn't need dawdling turtles to impede their pace.

Sometimes Jack pulled over as far as the snowy road edge would allow, to let hurried worriers pass. But mostly he kept going until he saw the sign:

Equamore. Its edges were decked out with sparkling white lights.

He got it. The words equine and amore. Horse love. That was their stated mission. He would see if the reality measured up.

Bouncing down the snowy but potholed gravel drive in the direction indicated by wooden arrows, he finally reached a long and tall covered-arena with an attached, lower-roofed stable. Two other vehicles were parked up near the big doors, buried to their hubcaps in new snow. If the snow began falling again, which it soon was supposed to, the hubcaps might disappear entirely.

That better not happen. It might quash the mission.

Jack parked and climbed out of the truck. He scrunched toward the doors, framed with white lights and evergreen boughs. The closer he came to the structure, the more he smelled warm horse and fresh alfalfa. There were none of the manure and urine smells one often smells at barns. Of course, maybe it was just the cold air keeping fumes at bay.

He slid open one barn door and stepped into a wide cement aisle flanked by iron-barred stalls. Horse's heads hung over the tops of some doors. Feed buckets or flakes of hay stood by, ready for the next feeding and watering. Christmas stockings filled with carrots hung from stall fronts. A few people dressed for the weather stood at the aisle's far end, some hundred feet down.

A slim woman in a cowboy hat, fleece jacket, tight jeans and muck boots separated herself from the group and walked toward him. After a few steps, she turned back and said something to a stout, cherub-cheeked woman, who blew an air kiss and gave her two thumbs up. When the first woman turned and again headed toward Jack, she poked at the enormous holly sprig stuck in her hat brim.

With a slight thrill Jack remembered she was the woman who'd smiled at him in the farm store checkout line. She had the same sparkling green eyes, accented by a sweep of dark mascara. And the same kind but no-nonsense air.

She reached him and extended her gloved right hand.

"Hi, Janine Bartell, director of Equamore. You must be Jack. Nice to meet you at last, Jack. But I feel I already know you." She cocked her head and studied him.

Bartell didn't remember him, then.

"Farm store? A week ago? I was waiting in line behind you?"

"Oh, yes. Sorry. I was buying a boatload of supplements. These rescue horses have a multitude of health issues. Especially the elderlies. Costs a small fortune to keep them going." She flashed a brittle smile.

An awkward silence passed between them. Jack didn't know what to say next.

But just as quickly Bartell's face softened. Her eyes shaded to friendly.

"Sorry for the misunderstanding, as I said last night. We are all about helping horses. And people, of course. We have at-risk teens here today, and might take on several as volunteers. We desperately need more. Our best girl quit. It's why I couldn't go out with you Saturday."

She gave Jack a sincere look. He'd have to buy that, for now.

"I see. Yes, I am sure this takes a lot of work." He glanced up and down the aisle. "Nice clean place you have."

"Thank you. So are you ready for us to go see your old horse on the Greensprings?"

"Oh, more than. I just hope he's made it through these last few days. Especially last night. I imagine it's been brutal up there."

They walked toward the barn doors.

"Those old ranch horses are tougher than they look. Especially if they've been out for a while. If he stays not far from the highway, as you say, he's smart. Just doing that sometimes keeps predators at bay."

"Yes, I thought of that," Jack nodded. But he walked more quickly, anxious for them to be on their way. Beyond the doors he saw the day had brightened but snow again had begun to fall. A dusting covered the tops of the vehicles, and a few horse trailers in the next lot.

Her gaze followed his. She lay a hand on his arm.

"I would take you on a tour of our facility, but I just finished showing the folks down the aisle around. We'd best get going if we're to get back in time. I have others coming after lunch."

Jack's shoulders dropped. He was under the impression this would be an all-day, or most-of-day, project, going out to see and hopefully rescue Survivor. Who knew if the old guy would let himself be caught, or if he did, how long it would take? You couldn't rush these things.

"Uh, all right. Whatever you wish, Ms. Bartell."

Carole T. Beers

"Call me Janine, as most people do. We aren't too formal here. We like to create a cozy home-farm atmosphere. That draws people in and keeps them coming back."

And keeps them in a mood to donate, Jack thought, with a prick of annoyance. For all her warmth and effectiveness, this Janine was also one tough cookie, who ruled with an iron fist in a kidskin glove. And expected others to do as asked.

Because of that, Equamore was a clean, well-lighted place for distressed horses, as well as for needy humans, and those hard-wired for helping. And you couldn't fault that.

Still, Jack felt doubt slither up his spine.

Carly

17.

Carly awoke late, and groggy. She pushed herself to a sitting position, wriggled off the couch and hobbled into the kitchen. Looking back, she smiled at seeing Mikey asleep with his stuffed horsie near the tree. One hand still held a half-eaten carrot.

The TV burbled in the background. "Sesame Street." There was Cookie Monster. Carly remembered that huge colorful guy with the enormous grin as a favorite when she was a few years younger.

After the excitement from the accident had died down, it had been a rather peaceful, almost smooth runup to Christmas. Only a few more days 'til Old Santa made his official appearance. She'd hit the Toys for Tots event, but still had a few more things to get.

The jolly elf, or his spiritual equivalent, already had given a kind of gift to Carly. In only a few days she'd learned to get around a bit with her hurt leg, and not had to lean too much on Daddy Jack. She didn't want him to jeopardize his job, although he reassured he wouldn't.

She'd had a call from Nate, too, just that morning. It was short and bittersweet.

"Just checking on you two," he said. "I feel responsible, having saved Mike and all."

Carly felt a jab of worry. She hoped the call was what he said, innocent, just checking up. But you never knew, with Nate. At least with the Nate she'd known.

"We're fine," she said coolly. "And you don't have to feel responsible. Let's just call it over and done with, and thank you for the help that night. Oh, and for the gift. Mikey spends every moment he can on that stuffed horse."

"Ha, I knew he'd like it. The minute it came into the store, I knew he had to have it. Maybe it was a premonition or something that made me go over that day."

Carly pondered those words. She wasn't sure she'd call his idea to come over with a gift, a premonition. He likely had been thinking of them before that. Would this encounter lead to more? Should she worry about stalking? Maybe borrow that .38 Derringer that her friend Suky had in her bedside table drawer?

Suky's ex had been a stalker. After they broke up, he'd begun calling her daily or several times a day, playing all innocent and helpful. Never made a threat, never lifted a finger or said a word to scare her. But just called, and "bumped" into her at odd times. Always made it sound like a coincidence, always had an explanation.

Suky had begun to have trouble sleeping. And that headline about an estranged husband going after his own wife and kids, burning down their house, had sent her over the edge. She'd gone out and bought a gun, taken a concealed-carry class and obtained the card allowing her to do so.

"Carly? You there?" Nate was saying now between bursts of static on the line.

"Oh," Carly said. "Yeah. Well, thanks for the call. But please don't call any more. Or come around. Daddy Jack was helping out, but I can drive now, and do my work although it takes longer. But we're OK."

She was tempted to end with, "Have a nice life," or something equally lame, but she remained silent.

Don't encourage him. Say as little as possible. Then hang up.

Which she did. She felt rude, but she felt it was the right thing to do. Nate would handle it. And if he didn't, oh well. That's how it was going to be.

A glance through the window showed it was snowing again. That might create problems for her going to her jobs tomorrow. She had a new one, in a hillier part of town. But it looked like a soft melty snow. No ice. She could do this.

She could do this, whatever it took. She felt she could do this, that is, until Mikey wriggled from his chair, ran into the living room and began to scream. Then to pound something against the floor.

Damn! That baby boy so needed real playtime, structured exercise, or some safe way to burn off his energy and fears so he'd stay relatively calm and in communication.

But in her condition, Carly couldn't get that done. At least for awhile.

And it was snowing again. She remembered what happened the last time he'd had a burst of unchannelled energy.

Jack

18.

Jack's hands tightened on the truck steering wheel. His foot hovered over the gas and brake. He was re-familiarizing himself with pulling an empty trailer.

The truck bucked as it alternately drew the rig over stretches of dry and ice-slick road. There wasn't much traffic, however, so progress was steady, if slow.

He and Janine Bartell from Equamore hadn't said spoken much since they'd hooked up the old white stock trailer at the stable, and tucked themselves into the cab for their mission on the mountain. Mainly about Jack's work and interests. Green lay curled between them on.

Jack offered Janine a sip of his coffee, still hot since he'd poured it at home less than an hour ago. But she, with a smile, declined, instead busying herself with a phone calls to past and future donors. Sometimes she jotted in a rainbow-cover notebook she'd pulled from her parka.

He drove a while more and then glanced over at her. She was involved in a yet another call, a least her fifth since they'd started up the pass highway. He'd hoped to have a decent conversation, talking about horses, the prospects for Survivor, things like that.

Oh, well I'm just happy she came. Gotta take what I can get.

At least she'd agreed to let him hitch up her ancient rescue trailer. The long, ratty rig, whose upper windowed-section let in a stiff wind and snow, was not a thing of beauty. But it should be up to the job of holding a half-wild horse. Especially with a bale of hay in the front corner to occupy the animal as it was trailered to the stable. Trailered, that is, if it could be persuaded to jump in the trailer. It easily could refuse.

Jack steered his mind away from such thoughts.

The wide spot in the highway where he'd parked before was thinly blanketed with snow. Jack feathered the brakes as he pulled over and parked well off the road. A couple other vehicles crawled by, their chains clanking or studded tires clicking, shooting a wake of slush and ice in their wake.

He put the truck in park, and scanned the meadow for the horse. "Stay here, Green," he told the dog. "We'll be back in a few." Then he climbed out of the cab, worry rising while he made his way through deep snow to the passenger side.

Janine held the passenger strap and stepped out, taking care not to slip. She turned her shoulder to a rising wind, and looked at Jack.

"Pretty brutal up here," she said, pulling her parka hood over her whipping hair. "Glad I dressed the part." She stamped her feet in the lug-sole rubber boots. "This is where the old guy hangs out? I don't see him. Sure this is the right place?"

Jack rubbed his gloved hands together. He tried to ignore the ice crystals stinging his cheeks. A worry furrow drew his eyebrows toward each other.

"He's gotta be around somewhere." He spoke with a confidence he did not feel. That old bronc had better show up. This might be his only chance.

"Sure hope so, Ma'am. Let's move closer to that bramble, the one that kind of looks like a train." Jack started to slip and slide down the short bank overlooking the meadow. "The horse sometimes takes cover there. Stays fairly close to the road, like you said. Pretty smart."

He motioned for Janine to follow, and offered a hand to help her down the bank.

She waved him away and made it down herself, picking her way through the snow, and stopping a few yards from the tangle of thorny canes.

Jack framed his mouth with his hands, and took a deep breath before yelling."Survivor! Hey, boy! You out here?"

He listened to the stillness, and then gave a sharp whistle. A flock of black-headed juncos, foraging in the outer ring of blackberry canes, flew up with a whir of wings. They sailed toward the road and settled along its tree-lined edge.

Jack whistled again.

Way across the snowfield, almost to the tree line, he saw movement. Small, but gratifying. It had to be the horse.

Jack whistled again. He prayed the old horse knew what he meant, and sensed they had come to help. Maybe he remembered the hay Jack had brought.

"Come on, boy!" Jack said. "Got more hay. Grain, too."

Janine pulled a pair of glasses from her pocket and put them on. She stared at the timber line where the faint outline of a snow-dusted equine became discernible.

"Definitely an old guy," Janine said, her glasses rims taking on a crust of snowflakes, and her boots sunk in snow. "Saw that from the pictures you sent. Looks even older in person. Sick, too. Mucus dripping."

"Been a hard winter." Jack brushed show off his shoulders, and shivered.

"I'll need a closer look, Jack. But to tell the truth? Not sure he'd be worth saving, much as I wish we could. Assuming we could get him to come closer."

Jack had to keep the positive tone moving.

"Well, he is old. But doggone tough," Jack said.

He words were swept away on a wind gust. Driven snowflakes stung his eyes. He turned his back to the wind. In the ten minutes they'd been there, icy damp began to penetrate his boots.

"He's sure enough tough," Janine shouted, starting back toward the truck and trailer. She trudged haltingly through the snow, stomping with each step to keep the soles free of packed ice. She looked to the road and back, and off to each side.

Jack watched her, his mind in turmoil. She must be very cold. What was she doing, going back to the truck? Was she done? She sure looked like she was.

His hope slipped a notch.

"Well, thank you for coming," he yelled after her. "Get warm in the truck and I'll keep trying to get him."

Almost to the vehicle, she waved a hand. "I'm good."

"Don't blame you if it seems too much," he said. "I know you have to get back."

She turned. "Glad to do it," she shouted as she looked down the road, where a red semi-truck labored through gears in the far lane.

The sounds it made were sudden, and rude, and invasive. Jack hoped they wouldn't scare the horse.

But the animal must have heard plenty of that in his years up here.

Jack trudged back up the slope and stood closer to Janine—so close that he caught a whiff of lemon cologne. It was a scent his wife used to wear, back when they were courting. It smelled good mixed with the odor of wet snow, bark and earth.

He hauled his thoughts back to the task at hand.

"Maybe I can talk you into coming again," he said. "When the snow stops. If he manages to live that long."

The minute he said the words, Jack knew there was no hope. He became aware his fingers were about to freeze. His legs felt like blocks of ice.

Hard as it was to get this kind woman out here with the trailer to take a look, it would be even harder to get her to come out a second time. Wasn't in the cards. Jack took her arm. She turned to look at him. He couldn't read her look. But her body had a purposeful rigidity.

"I hate taking you up here on a wild goose chase," he said. "It's getting late. I'll take you on back."

She thought for a moment, and then shook her head, her eyes serious. She looked again over the meadow. She let out a heavy breath and looked at him. "Thank you, Jack. I'm a busy woman, and this is one of our busiest times of year. He seems to be getting by all right."

Jack looked away. He watched his breath clouds drifting in the now-still arctic air.

So it is not to be.

Jack

19.

Janine Bartell move closer to Jack as they stood watching the old horse out in the snow. Her arm touched his. "Do you have all-wheel drive?"

"I do." What was that about? They'd made it up here all right with an empty trailer, just like they would make it back home.

"Drive up the highway to where it's a more gradual a drop, where the field is higher," she said. "Back the trailer as far as you can down toward the bramble."

Jack couldn't believe it. Was she saying they should still try to get the horse? He gave her a questioning look.

"Well?" she said, a smile warming her eyes.

"I could try that I guess. Don't hurt to try." His eyes searched hers.

"Hurry, now. While the horse is still there and can see us."

Jack was stunned by what seemed a sudden change of heart. His eyelashes dampened but he told himself it was from the snow. "Right. I'm on it."

Suddenly oblivious to the cold, he quickly moved around the truck, got in and fired up the engine. His dog whined when exhaust belched into the air.

Jack inched the rig halfway onto the road, and out about fifty more feet along the gritty snow shoulder.

Janine walked ahead down the edge of the road to where she wanted him to back, then stepped aside and nodded.

He hoped she was right, and that the incline would support the truck and trailer. He didn't know what footing he'd find when he reached the meadow.

The incline was perfect, and the meadow under the snow was solid.

But he took it slow. Lightly touched the gas and brake pedals, turning the wheels slightly this way and that, keeping the motion going. His palms sweated inside his work gloves.

In a few minutes, trailer and truck were backed down about forty feet from the bramble, in clear sight of the horse at the tree line.

Jack turned off the ignition and stepped from the truck. His feet stood on frozen ground under the piled snow and mat of meadow grass. Ahead the bramble seemed more imposing. A good hundred feet long and twenty feet wide. Lots of cover for critters big and small. What a wonder of nature.

"Now, Jack."

Her voice startled him. His worry had been replaced with a little hope.

"Yeah."

"Get a few flakes of hay from the trailer and spread it out beyond the bramble. I'll take a halter and rope. Then put grain in the bucket. We'll rattle it. They usually get the picture."

Jack did as instructed, trying not to count too much on a happy outcome. He went to the back of the trailer. The door resisted opening, and then gave a rusty creak.

He took a full armload of alfalfa against his chest. He cursed himself for not brining the snowshoes, but thought he could make it. Glad for something constructive to do, he marched with the hay to the edge of the bramble and scattered hay in a trail toward the horse It was a lot of hay. The horse had to see that.

Even if the animal did not come today, he at least would have something to eat for a few more days. At least until the storm broke. This trip would not be entirely wasted.

Janine came toward Jack with the old green halter and cotton lead rope slung over her left shoulder. She held the steel bucket by its handle in her right hand, and rattled the grain inside as she walked to the end of the hay trail. She stopped, and shook the bucket some more.

Ratttle, rattle.

They waited, watching and listening. The horse had not moved. If anything it looked farther away.

At least ten more minutes passed. The sky seemed to brighten. Not much, but enough.

"I don't think he's coming," Jack said.

"Maybe not. But he knows darn well what's happening. He's thinking it over."

Jack marveled at Janine's knowledge of horses. It shouldn't be otherwise. It was her calling, after all. He prided himself on being sensitive to others' thoughts and feelings, having raised a passel of foster kids and pets. Hell, having just lived sixty decades. But Janine Bartell clearly was his equal in discerning.

Another five minutes passed.

Then the horse let out a long snort, shook his head, and finally left the timber, plodding up the meadow toward them. He looked like he hurt. His head bobbed whenever his right front hoof hit the ground. But still he kept coming. Slow but steady.

Jack held his breath.

The animal stopped and raised his head. He scented the air, stared long at them. A stiffness seemed to come over his body. He raised his head, and took a half-step sideways.

Looking for escape routes, Jack thought. Just in case.

"Hope he keeps coming," Jack whispered.

Janine remained silent. She pressed her lips together, and looked down at her feet. She scuffed her boots in the snow.

Jack took these as an indication of her impatience. "How long should we wait? You have to get back."

"Yes. Let's go get in the truck. It'll be warmer there."

"Shall I get your bucket?" He looked at where it sat at the end of the hay.

"Let's leave it." She turned and walked back to the truck. Jack followed closely. His heart felt heavy.

They climbed into the cab and closed the doors against the wind, again rising. Green nudged his sleeve.

Jack patted him. "Good boy. Need to get out?" The dog lay his head back down. The next second, Jack turned the key in the ignition, and turned on the heater. "Guess we'd best get going."

Janine put her gloved hand on Jack's. "No."

He looked at her, confused.

She tapped her window. "Look. Here he comes."

Jack peered past her. Sure enough, the old horse was walking steadily now toward the bramble, eyes on the bucket and the line of hay across the snow.

"I don't believe it," breathed Jack, a grin breaking through his still-chilled face. A warm feeling spread through him. "I'll be damned. Here he comes."

They watched the horse stop again ten feet from the bucket. He stretched out his nose, and sniffed, sending up spouts of breath. He raised his head and looked at the truck and trailer. Then he lowered his head and moved forward.

The next moment his nose was deep in the bucket.

"There," Janine said. "We've got him. The rest should be easy."

Jack was not so sure. But he was willing to believe anything this woman now said.

"Shall I go get him, or do you want to?"

"Both. You get out first, slowly, and make sure the trailer door is open. He knows you. Then lay more hay from this end of the bramble and on into the trailer."

Jack did as he was told. He dared not doubt or do more thinking of any kind. He just wanted this to happen.

He stood to one side of the trailer door, a few feet away, in view of the horse. Janine approached the animal. She talked softly, as she went. Jack couldn't hear her words, but saw Survivor briefly lift his head from the bucket, chew a moment and then go back to his feast.

Janine walked right up to him and laid the rope over his neck. When he raised his head again, she slowly slipped the halter on it. Then she led him to the hay.

He ate hungrily, blowing softly now and then to clear his nostrils of chaff and hay dust. He showed no sign of fear or nervousness. It was as if he'd done this all his life.

Jack thought he probably had.

"Make sure the door doesn't blow in the wind," said Janine, tugging on the lead rope.

The horse stepped forward with her, dropping his head again and again to snatch big mouthfuls of hay.

She led him steadily toward the trailer, paused at the step without looking back, let him stick his head in the trailer to check it out. Then she mounted the step. He followed as if he'd done that all his life.

Jack closed the door, but did not latch it. He heard Janine reassuring and patting the horse before tying his rope to the bar in the front of the trailer. Then she pushed open the door, turned around and latched it.

"Let's go," she told Jack. "Good job."

The horse neighed once, and stomped inside the trailer, and gave a long snort.

Then Jack heard munching sounds.

At that moment he became aware that the sight and sound of a large safe animal eating, and at a confident, leisurely pace, was one of life's great comforts and joys. Especially if Jack had a hand in that comfort.

It meant that at that time and in that particular place, all was right with their world.

Carly

20.

Carly drove with her hands lightly on the steering wheel, listening to a new Western tune on the beater car she'd bought for five-hundred dollars. Occasionally she sipped creamed coffee from a kiosk cup, or kept time to the music by tapping her purple fingernails on the wheel.

It was good to have a day off work, be out in the country. But there were still slippery spots, so she kept one eye on the rearview and one on the road winding through the farmland.

She was about twenty minutes into her journey to the address Daddy Jack had given her. He wouldn't say whose it was, or why he'd summoned her. That was part of the surprise, he'd said. Don't want to spoil it, he'd said.

Whatever. He likes a game. If I can trust anyone, I can trust him.

The sun finally had come out to melt the snow and ice this Christmas Eve day. Wintering birds hopped and scratched by the side of the road, reminding her of this morning when she'd spread peanut butter on a pine cone for the junco outside her window. Almost immediataely he summoned his flock.

It gave her a surprisingly warm feeling to help an animal. It was not something Carly was used to doing.

Up to now she'd mainly helped people. Animals still somewhat mystified her.

So far it had been a peaceful drive. Little Mike had fussed in his rear-facing car seat when they set off. But he was quiet now. She was happy about that since her late-night job shift had been especially tough. Carly was still getting used to walking on her damaged leg.

The radio crackled with static. She changed it to a soft rock station.

She flinched at a sudden shriek from the back seat. Glancing in the rearview, she saw Mikey's hands were fists pumping straight out and up from his sides. They were not keeping-time pumps, but upset and angry ones.

She changed the station back to country, guessing the music change had set him off.

Damn. He's been doing so well.

She drove on, saying a small prayer. But the boy grew increasingly fretful behind her. He grunted and squealed in a spiraling tempo, momentarily falling silent but the starting up again. His pounding fists and feet drowned out the sound of the music.

"Umm, pooh, umh!" he yelled.

Usually soft music soothed the child. Not this time. Mikey's booted feet beat the back seat, shocking Carly each time they hit. She should have put tennis shoes on him. But Daddy Jack had insisted both of them wear boots and dress for winter, wherever this meeting was supposed to take place.

Daddy Jack had been unusually mysterious about it all. The only thing he'd said was, "It might change your life, and in a good way."

Carly didn't have a clue what he'd meant. But he'd been insistent. Whatever it was he'd wanted to show her, couldn't wait. So it must be really important. At least she'd had time on her way through town to make a quick stop for something she desperately needed.

She slowed the car so she could read addresses on mailboxes, which were few and farther between, the more miles she drove.

Another "Bam! Bam!" on the seat behind made Carly turn away from the wheel.

"Mikey! Stop it!"

The car swerved. It raced toward the ditch. But time slowed like stretching hot toffee.

Carly whipped her attention back forward and wrenched the wheel. The car jerked away from its path toward the ditch, but lurched into oncoming traffic. Heart pounding, she fought to regain control. The next second they were headed straight again.

She blew out a sigh. They were safe. They'd have Christmas.

The boy's noise had stopped at the sudden action of the car. His banging had subsided. But he began to whimper.

Carly was working on a headache. Grabbing her cup from the console, she gulped coffee.

Late in the day for coffee. I can't tolerate it after noon. But I'm tired and stressed.

Looking back again, she saw Mikey straining and picking at the harness supposed to keep him safe. It was a new design, courtesy of Daddy Jack, an early Christmas present to them the previous day.

Carly knew the harness would hold, even a kid as strong as Mikey. But she also knew it could leave bruises if he thrashed too much. His old one had done that. Having had a gruelling night diapering, feeding and toiletting her disabled client, she was in no mood to tend any wounds Mikey might sustain today.

"Please, Lord," she murmured, "just help me get through this."

She flashed on what an up-and-down holiday it had been. Her studying for her test, and Mikey having setbacks. Her passing the test and getting jobs, then having Mikey almost hit by that car, and her suffering a concussion and sprained ankle.

Finally, Nate's reappearance in her life. That still troubled her. Why could she not stop thinking about that? At least he had not called again or worse, shown up. That was something.

Another "bam-bam" from the car's back seat.

"Mikey? You OK?" Carly felt guilty for concentrating on negative things so much, this day before Christmas. She should be positive, as least for Mikey's sake. His life was tough enough. Never mind, her life with him.

Carly

21.

As she drove, slower now, the sun-warmed pavement nearly bare of snow, Carly saw a lighted brown sign with white lettering come into view across the road twenty yards ahead. It stood above a corner where two sections of three-rail brown fencing met.

Pastures inside the fences were empty, snow still standing in shaded areas. Beyond them lay an open riding arena, and two long stables set at right angles to each other with what looked like a covered arena at the meeting of both angles.

Carly rechecked the address she'd written down, and turned into the gravel drive. It ended at the stable to her right, where a half-dozen cars and Daddy Jack's truck sat.

She got out, careful not to slip on the muddy ground, and helped Mikey out of his car seat. He was curiously still and silent. He stared dully at the stable doors when one slid open.

Daddy Jack peered out. Then the man himself, illuminated by sunshine, came to stand in the open doorway. "See you made it, Carl. Beginning to worry. Come in. It's warmer inside."

Carly took Mikey's mittened hand and led him to the door.

"What's this all, about?" she said.

"You'll see," he said.

Inside, she hugged Daddy Jack and held up Mikey.

"How ya doin', Mister Mike?" The man took the boy, kissed his cheek and carried him down the aisle flanked by stall fronts. Horse heads stuck out over half doors, and whinnies or snorts greeted the trio's passage toward the far end.

Two middle-aged women stood down there. The slim, nicer looking one walked briskly forward, hand outstretched. A smile brightened her face and her eyes glowed with delight.

"Hello. Janine Bartell. You must be Carly. Welcome to Equamore. A forever home for special horses. Nice to meet you. Jack's told me so much about you, and Mike."

She gave Carly a light hug while Jack set the boy down on the floor.

"Um," said Carly. "Nice to meet you, too." Carly was beyond puzzled. Who was this woman and why were they here? How did Jack know her?

"This must be Mike," said Janine, bending down to take the boy's hand. "Hello, Mike. Jack has told me so much about you. I hope you are ready for your big happy Christmas surprise."

Mikey stared blankly at her. A bead of saliva clung to his lower lip but threatened to drop.

"Say, 'Hello, nice to meet you," Carly prompted, giving him a nudge.

Mikey said nothing, and continued to stare at the unknown woman.

Jack stepped up to take Mikey's other hand. "How's my big boy? Ready for Santa?"

Mikey only looked around, taking in horses sticking their heads out of stall openings. The boy's gaze came to rest on face of a grizzled red-brown horse in the stall to his immediate left.

The horse tossed his head and returned Mikey's gaze. A moment of recognition seemed passed between them. Or so Carly believed. Isn't that how things happened in movies with animals? The horse reminded her of that rusty toy by the Pennington steps. The little horse always looked like it was running away from something. Or like Carly, running *to* something, trying get out of present cold reality and into a better life.

Mikey shook his hands limply, over and over. Carly was about to stop him when he pointed at the animal. "Horsie?"

Carly couldn't believe her ears. Had she heard right? "Horsie, yes." She bit her lower lip and looked at Daddy Jack, who smiled. "What's this all about, Daddy Jack? Why are we here? What's going on?"

"Keep watching, Carl, and learning." Daddy Jack pulled a carrot by its green top from the felt Christmas stocking on the stall door. "I rescued the old horse I told you about, Survivor here, and then got this wild idea how he might help us."

"Help us? How would that work?"

Jack inclined his head toward the boy, who stood transfixed by the horse.

The sight of the carrot brought the animal up to the stall bars. He poked his nose between the uprights. He wiggled his lips.

Little Mike gave a happy shriek. He leaped forward, and dashed in his toddler way to the stall. Hands stretched and fingers wiggling, he looked at Carly. A smile filled his entire face.

"Horsie! Horsie!"

He turned back toward the stall and reached to an opening between bars. He alternately spread and clamped his fingers, ran his tongue around his lips, and jabbed his hand toward the horse's nose.

Survivor snorted and jerked up his head. As if slapped, he jumped back at the boy's sudden action. He shook his head as if to say, "I don't like that."

Mikey lowered his hand. Frowning, he turned to look at his mother.

Carly, shocked yet strangely hopeful, opened her mouth to tell him to move more slowly. To watch the horse, look for what it might be telling him, and let it come to him. Speak softly.

She almost told him those things. But she hesitated.

Where did I learn that? Is it even right? And will Mikey understand?

She looked over at Daddy Jack, and held up her palms.

He nodded enthusiastically, and pointed to the boy.

Carly was astounded by what she saw. Mikey was sliding his hand ever so slowly up the half-wall toward the stall bars. The stable was as quiet as church when people were praying.

Survivor blew gently, and watched Mikey. Then the horse took a slow step forward.

Daddy Jack put the carrot he was holding into the boy's dimpled hand. "Give him a carrot to eat, Mike. Car-rot. To horsie, it's a cookie."

When the youngster grabbed it, Daddy Jack lifted the child's hand and demonstrated how to hold the carrot horizontally at a space between stall bars. He opened Mikey's hand so the carrot lay across the palm. "Hold it this way, fingers tight and flat," he said, looking first at Mike, and then at Carly. This lesson was for her, as well. "That way you keep the horse's teeth from biting your finger."

Mikey stared at Daddy Jack, as if uncomprehending. Then he turned back to the horse in the stall, reached higher, and tried to keep his outstretched, trembling hand with the carrot flat and steady at the bars.

"Like dis?" Mikey said over his shoulder.

Carly gasped at hearing the boy's coherent, comprehending words. Her knees weakened.

Daddy Jack leaned down to whisper, "Yes, son. Do like I said. Go on."

Survivor's ears flicked forward and back. His nostrils flared. He took a step toward the bars. Planted that foot, transferred his weight. Then he took another step.

"Talk to him…Mike," Carly urged. It occurred to her it might be time to address her boy by his real name. Daddy Jack, Nate, too, called him Mike. "Talk gentle," she added, "like I talk to you when you're scared." She patted the boy's shoulder. It felt so small, warm, precious.

"Here, Horsie," crooned Mike. "Want dis?" He held his hand steady outside the bars.

At hearing that, seeing him reach out to the horse, Carly's eyes watered. She sniffled, and looked at Daddy Jack. He folded his arms and beamed. Janine Bartell was smiling, too.

Carole T. Beers

Survivor stretched his neck. His whiskery lips nuzzled the carrot. Some whiskers touched Mike's hand.

"Eeee! Tickles!" Mike's hand quivered but stayed at the bars.

Suddenly the whole carrot disappeared into Survivor's mouth. Mike's hand jerked away as if burned. The boy tilted his head.

Feeling like she was standing in a tunnel, Carly heard only muffled crunching. She saw only Mike's empty hand reaching toward Survivor's muzzle, dribbling foam with carrot flecks.

Mike giggled and pointed. "He like," he exclaimed. "Horsie like. Caw-wot. Cay-wat."

"Yes, he does," said Carly. "He likes the carrot. He likes you, too, Mike."

The boy looked up at her and then back at the horse. He bounced on his toes.

In the aisle behind them, Janine softly applauded. "Bravo." The red-cheeked older woman he'd seen earlier with Janine, now moved out from the shadows down the aisle.

"Did you see that, Gwen? I think we've got a winner."

Gwen sauntered up to Janine and put an arm around her waist. "Good job, Jan."

Daddy Jack smiled over at the women, and then at Carly. He folded his arms. His blue eyes sparkled with mischief.

"I'm thinking this old boy can kind of be Mike's horse," he said. "And yours, too, Carl. If you want to come visit him now and then."

Carly was puzzled. "I'm kind of scared of horses."

- 116 -

"He's a good boy. Look how he appreciates all this attention. He's real quiet, it turns out. Exactly what Mike needs. I know something about autism. Look at what just happened."

"I know, but—"

"Be good for both of you. Janine tells me that structured interaction with horses does a world of good for special-needs kids. Their caregivers, too. You can bring Mike often as you want. Who knows, even ride this old guy one day, with someone leading you."

Janine, who'd been standing in the background, moved up between Carly and Jack. She lay a hand on each one's shoulder, and crinkled her eyes.

"Jack is right, Carly. Your son and this old horse can share special moments, tell each other secrets, learn trust, confidence. We're happy to facilitate. It will be good for you, too."

"You can help each other...survive," Jack interjected.

While thinking about this, trying to keep the good vibe going, Carly leaned down to stroke a black cat rubbing against her calves. "I like the idea. But I'm not sure we can afford a horse. I know they're really expensive." She straightened, and looked down the aisle.

"It's not really your horse," Janine said. "So don't worry about that. We'll do all the care, because we rescue animals for life. But it can be your and Mike's horse in every other way." She smiled. "Thanks to Daddy Jack."

"And, as I said," Jack put in, "I will help some financially. Gonna be tight, with my not working. But I think I could swing twenty bucks a month, help clean the stall. I'lll have more time in a week or so. Might

Carole T. Beers

even talk my wife into showing Mike how to groom the horse."

"Hmm, interesting," said Carly. "It would do Mama Ellen good, maybe help her deal with pain and balance issues. Didn't she used to ride?"

"She did," Jack beamed. "Pretty good at it, too."

"By all means, have her come," Janine said. "The more the merrier."

Little Mike watched their interchange as if it were a ping-pong match. "Horsie, he said, turning back to the stall. He stroked Survivor's nose, poking through the bars for more treats. "Good horsie."

Carly finally knew why Daddy Jack had insisted they come here today. He'd guessed this old horse could play a big role in Mike's life—a calming, empowering role. A friend without words. An equal who communicated with trust but no judgment. Something alive and warm Something his very own. Which was a kind of gift to Carly, as well.

"Thanks, Daddy Jack," she said, taking his arm and pecking his grizzled cheek.

He twinkled. "Hey. Thank Survivor. And Equamore."

They embraced. Carly didn't want to let go.

She called Nate at the farm store that afternoon. She told him what had happened with Mike and Daddy Jack at Equamore, of what she considered a breakthrough for Mike, and their plans regarding Equamore. She owed him that.

It was like talking to an old friend—easy, natural, strangely comforting.

Nate wanted to celebrate by taking her and Mike to lunch the next day before they went to Equamore again. To put Carly at ease, he'd ask Daddy Jack and Mama Ellen along.

This time Carly didn't hesitate. She would take care, and take her time, but probably let Nate back into their life in some way. After all. Mike needed to know his father.

Bad luck, bad choices, could be turned around. She—and Survivor—were living proof.

Jack

22.

That evening at home, Jack had just finished opening his gifts from under the tree, and watching his wife opens hers. He drained the last of his hot cocoa with two drops of bourbon. This was Christmas, after all.

He watched Wilhelm gnaw on a new treat bone between his paws on a pile of crumpled paper and ribbon. He chuckled when Green nosed a plastic ornament across the mess, tossed it in the air and scampered after it, catching it cleanly in his jaws. And did it again and again.

Hey, if no one will play with you, you make up your own game.

Finishing the cocoa, Jack got up and walked to Ellen's recliner. He grinned, reaching down to pat her arm.

"Merry Christmas, hon," he said. "I have so many blessings. You among them.."

She'd been lost in thought, staring at the tree. She turned toward him, her features soft. "I'm so glad your mission yesterday was successful." She shook back her hair. She'd put on black mascara and baby-pink lipstick. She smelled of rosewater.

"You look nice," Jack said. "Been meaning to tell you."

She reddened, but held his gaze. "Thank you."

"I would like you to come out with me some time soon to see that old horse. Maybe when Mike and Carly go. The lady said you might enjoy grooming him? Show Mike how? Maybe after a while even put the boy up on the horse, lead it around?"

Her eyes searched Jack's. Then a glow spread over her face.

"Why, what an excellent idea, Jack. I would really love that."

"You would?"

"I'd been thinking of a way to get back into horses, and the out of doors. It would be good exercise. How about tomorrow, if they're open?"

"I think they are," Jack said. "Then it's a date."

He squeezed her arm, creaked himself up to a standing position, and padded back to his recliner. With one smooth move he sat down and tilted the back to his liking. Then he adjusted his feet on the outstretched footrest.

He wiggled his toes inside his plush new sheepskin slippers. The quality, hard-soled kind. The hundred-dollar kind. Pendletons.

I always wanted a pair of those. That Carly kid is just about the best. Raised her right.

*. *. *

MEET OUR AUTHOR
Carole T. Beers

Carole T. Beers

Born in Portland, Ore., to descendants of Oregon Trail pioneers, Carole T. Beers fell in love with writing as soon as she could read, and with horses as soon as she could ride. After earning a B.A. in Journalism at University of Washington, she taught at private schools, wrote for romance magazines and worked for 32 years as a reporter/critic for the Pulitzer Prize-winning Seattle Times newspaper. Several of her pieces won awards. Along the way she competed on a women's shooting team and earned a pilot's license. She also worked in marketing and retail—great sources of story and character ideas!

Carole now lives in Southern Oregon where she writes "New West Mysteries with Heart." These include the fast, fun Pepper Kane novels featuring a spirited ex-reporter who shows Western horses, sells tack, and solves crimes with the aid of her Lakota-police partner, Sonny Chief. Set in the Pacific Northwest but sometimes venturing into the Southwest, her books showcase Carole's love of nature, time spent with animal or human friends, mind-teasing puzzles and hopeful endings.

Soon Carole will publish a novella, "The Stone Horse," inspired by Zuni carvings of spirit animals. Years ago she mentored Indian youth, sang on a drum and danced in pow-wows with the support of Lakota, Cree and Northwest Coast friends. She still holds these friendships dear to her heart.

Her free-time pursuits include dancing, hiking, playing games and watching the Seattle Seahawks with her husband, Richard. She also likes to attend Bethany Presbyterian Church, hang with her Boston Terriers and ride her American Paint horse, Shiny Good Bar ("Brad"). Though retired from showing, she still rides as if she may show next week.

Reach Carole on her website. http://www.caroletbeers.com or her Facebook:http://www.facebook.com/caroletbeersauthor

Kindly leave an honest review of this book at www.Amazon.com and www.Goodreads.com

Made in the USA
Lexington, KY
21 November 2019